# A BOOK TO KILL FOR

A Bookish Cafe Mystery Book 1

HARPER LIN

M aggie Bell darted from doorway to doorway, trying to escape the rain as she struggled with her umbrella. No matter how hard she pressed the button, the contraption would not unfold and protect her from the elements. Instead, like a wet moth fresh from its cocoon, it remained folded up tight.

It was a strange morning. All the parking spaces in which she would have normally parked were full, so she practically had to walk from the other side of town to her job. Somewhere down Agatha Street, she remembered she put her coffee mug on the top of her car before getting in. This was the third mug she'd lost in the past six months. But there was also a shift in the air, like something was going to happen but hadn't decided when. Maggie blamed it on her nasty attitude and the desire to go back home, crawl back under the covers, and call in sick.

"Oh, come on," she moaned as she shook her umbrella.

Drier passersby gawked at her, but she barely noticed, since her black-framed glasses were covered in drops of water. When she looked through them, she had the compound vision of a fly. After taking a deep breath from the safety of the Old

Cedar Bank doorway, she looked up into the sky. It was a swirling mess of gray clouds. The wind wasn't strong, but it was enough to direct the drops right in her direction. She spied another doorway across the street at the Spotlight Boutique that would offer a couple inches of shelter.

After looking both ways to make sure traffic was clear, she hurried off the sidewalk and splashed into a puddle that went up to her ankle. She cried out a very unladylike word. Finally, she reached the Spotlight Boutique doorway. She had to press her back into it, as it didn't provide the shelter she'd hoped for.

It took another ten minutes for Maggie to get to her place of employment. She leapt over two giant gray puddles and wove among the scattering of pedestrians who proudly displayed their working, manageable umbrellas before she reached the glass front door through which she'd been entering almost every day for over six years.

The words "*Whitfield Bookshop*" were painted on the glass in chipped and scratched gold letters, the hours of business below them. The little sign hanging there read "Closed," but Maggie knew the door was open. Mr. Whitfield had always left it open for her. Plus, it wasn't as if the people of Fair Haven, Connecticut, were busting down the door to buy a good book. They wouldn't know a good book if it sprouted teeth and bit them on the hind end.

"Is that you, Mags?" Mr. Whitfield called from high up in the back of the store.

"Yes," Maggie grumbled. She dumped her useless umbrella in the garbage can and shook her head, letting droplets fall everywhere. She squinted down the row of books and gasped.

"Alexander Whitfield, what are you doing up on that ladder? If I've told you once, I've told you a thousand times: just wait for me to get here!" Maggie hurried up to her boss, who was in his seventies, and helped him get down from his perch.

"I'm not crippled," he barked.

"Fine. When you fall off the ladder and crack your head open, don't come running to me," Maggie replied.

"I had to put *The Olive Tree* back in its proper place," he muttered with his chin held high. "You finished it in three days. A three-hundred-plus-page book. I thought I'd have more time. Oh, what happened to you? Didn't you hear the weather for today? They've been calling for rain all week."

"Yeah, I heard the weather," she replied as she pulled off her soaked sweater, walked over to the kitchenette next to Mr. Whitfield's cubby, and wrung it out.

"Don't you have an umbrella?" Mr. Whitfield asked innocently. "You know, I have a half dozen of them. People leave them behind all the time."

"I had one," she grumbled. "But it broke. The button wouldn't work."

"Ah, there's your problem. Plastic buttons and flimsy material certainly won't work for you. Now, on your way home, you will take this." Mr. Whitfield hobbled over to his desk and pulled an elegantly carved hook handle from a tall brass canister. It was attached to a long umbrella with silver-tipped ribs and thick vinyl webbing.

After wiping off her glasses, Maggie walked over and looked at what Mr. Whitfield was holding. It was an old umbrella. When she held it in her hand, she could tell, because it was heavy, made of real metal and wood.

"This will protect you. And keep it with you, because the rain is not expected to stop for the next several days." Mr. Whitfield reached under the flaps of vinyl, showed Maggie where to press the metal tab down, and then gently glided the ring all the way up to the top. The umbrella bloomed like a black flower.

HARPER LIN

"Mr. Whitfield, it's bad luck to open an umbrella indoors," Maggie said.

"Oh, posh. Here." He slid the umbrella closed and handed it to Maggie with a wink. "Now, put this away. What do we have on the agenda for today?"

"You were going to finish my monthly list," Maggie said as she took the umbrella, delicately touching the etched handle and admiring the silver tip.

"Have you finished all the books I gave you from last month?" Mr. Whitfield asked.

"You know I did." Maggie rolled her eyes as she followed behind him after tucking the umbrella behind the small counter at which she spent most every day. "You say that every time you have to give me a new list."

"Which one was your favorite?" Mr. Whitfield asked as he took a seat behind his small desk. It was covered with papers and notes, receipts and bills, rubber bands, sticky pads, and a large stack of used envelopes with stamps he found charming bound with a piece of red yarn. There was also an assortment of vintage pens in various stages of dryness that often required him to lick the tip to get the ink to flow.

"We discussed this already, Mr. Whitfield. I told you that *The Count of Monte Cristo* was my favorite out of this bunch. I'm glad I saved it for last, because *Madam Bovary* was…" Maggie pretended to yawn and stretch her mouth wide while patting it with her hand.

"But what of the main character, Emma Bovary?" Mr. Whitfield asked as he took a seat and pulled out a sheet of paper.

"Ugh. I really didn't care for her," Maggie replied.

"Just because she wanted love and to be loved?" Mr. Whitfield asked.

"She was a bore and ignorant by choice. Not to mention no one is going to buy the cow if the milk is free. That isn't a saying that just popped up when I was a kid. She had to know

4

that too," Maggie joked, and she smiled as Mr. Whitfield laughed.

Just then, a sleek black cat crossed in front of Mr. Whitfield's desk and came right up to Maggie, slinking affectionately around her legs.

"Poe, you agree with me, don't you?" Maggie asked the cat as she picked him up. She felt his tail happily whipping against her side as she placed him on Mr. Whitfield's desk.

"Speaking of which, do you have any plans this evening? A date perhaps?" Mr. Whitfield asked. He searched for a pen, licked the tip, and began to write notes on a pink Post-it.

"Speaking of giving the milk away for free... No, I don't have a date. Are you nuts?" Maggie huffed. "Everyone I meet, Mr. Whitfield, pales in comparison to you."

"Oh, posh. Maggie, I worry about you. I'm not going to be around forever. You can't waste your life hanging around an old coot like me," he said as he wrote.

"I can be myself around you, Mr. Whitfield. No one else in all of Fair Haven wants to talk about books or even reads. It's what I love. And no one wants to know about it, so it's pretty safe to assume they don't want to know about me."

"That isn't true. You're just shy," Mr. Whitfield said.

After a deep breath, Maggie shrugged. "I don't know how to talk to people."

"You talk to me just fine," he added.

"Yeah, but that's because you're just a crazy bookworm. It's easy to talk to you," Maggie said as she stroked Poe's head and felt the vibration of his purring.

"You have more to offer than you think, Margaret Bell. Any man would be lucky to scoop up a young lady like you," Mr. Whitfield said. "Now, I'll read you your list for this month. I expect you to take all month reading them. Don't finish all ten books this week."

When Maggie had first been hired by Mr. Whitfield six years earlier, he had seen firsthand her severely introverted nature. She was the perfect candidate to work in his bookstore, as he was introverted too. But their mutual love of books had eventually brought her out of her shell—at least where Mr. Whitfield was concerned—and he began to care for her like a daughter.

So they slowly got to know one another. Mr. Whitfield, who had read almost every book in his secondhand and vintage bookstore, which boasted more than five thousand titles, would give Maggie a list of books to read for the month. They were all on the shelves. Some of them were old and forgotten by almost everyone but their authors, and others were classics Maggie had read several times. This was what she'd do most days as the hours ticked by. Customers at the bookshop were rare, since the store did not carry the latest young-adult vampire series or comic books.

"What is the first title?" Maggie smiled and was eager to know the first book Mr. Whitfield had in mind for her to read.

"*The Streets of Laredo*. Westerns. McMurtry," Mr. Whitfield called out to her.

She walked down three rows of books that went from floor to ceiling to the Western section. She found the book, and her eyes sparkled; she loved westerns. Although she would never admit it to anyone, she loved how the men were so masculine and had no qualms stealing a long, passionate kiss from their fair lady before leaving to find gold or chase down the man from a Wanted poster.

"Found it! What's next?" she called. But there was no answer. "Mr. Whitfield? Don't leave me on tenterhooks!" She chuckled. But still there was no reply. Maybe the phone had rung and he was talking. But she hadn't heard it ring. Maybe he was changing his mind and writing down another title.

With her book held tightly in one hand, Maggie slowly walked back toward Mr. Whitfield's cubby, where she saw him sitting.

"Mr. Whitfield, are you all right?" she asked.

But still he didn't reply. He made no movement at all. When she looked at his face, it was as if he'd fallen asleep and was just peacefully dreaming at his desk.

Maggie put her hand on his shoulder and gave him a gentle shake.

His hand fell to his side, dropping the list of books she was to read this month.

He was dead.

## Chapter 2

The smell Maggie noticed throughout the Pearlman Family Funeral Home was not unpleasant. It was lemony. There was a lot of hardwood throughout the place, and Maggie wondered how long it took Mr. Pearlman to polish everything, because there wasn't a speck of dust anywhere. Boxes of tissues sat on every table, along with a couple bowls filled with peppermints. She'd tossed a few into her pocket but didn't eat any. Her stomach couldn't handle having anything in it.

Even though Maggie had made all the arrangements for the funeral, she felt like an interloper. It was nice to see so many people from the town show up to say good-bye. They chatted with Maggie, telling her what a nice man her boss had been and how they'd miss him. A few people asked if she'd be taking over the bookstore, but before she could form a proper response, they moved on to chat with someone else more interesting.

So Maggie stood by herself near the head of the casket and quietly whispered to Mr. Whitfield. She wished he were alive to see the crowd he had drawn. He'd have laughed at all the people who showed up. But Maggie wasn't surprised. She knew Mr. Whitfield had led a secret life of doing good. He'd dropped off crates of food for poor families on the other end of town every Thanksgiving. At some of the restaurants in town, during Christmas, he'd pay the tabs of large families or maybe a couple just starting out. The animal shelter received bags of dog and cat food anonymously donated year-round. Maggie saw some of the receipts, but she never said anything. If he'd wanted her to know, he'd have told her. The thought that these things would be missing this year broke her heart.

But she choked back the tears. The last thing she wanted was to attract attention to herself. It was bad enough that she felt like the only person who had dressed up. A vintage black cardigan and a long pleated black skirt weren't hard to throw together. As she looked around, she saw blue jeans and khakis and yoga pants. Really? Yoga pants?

"Maggie? Maggie?"

It was Roger Hawes. He was wearing baggy blue Carhartt work pants and a button-down shirt that looked like he'd been wearing it for the past few days. He always looked like this.

"Yes, Roger?" Maggie asked.

"I'm assuming that you know about Alex's finances. I'm wondering when he plans on selling the place." Roger's cheeks were red, and he was slightly out of breath, as if he'd been running.

"Roger, I don't know any of the particulars at this time. Mr. Whitfield only passed two days ago and…"

"You know why I'm asking. I've made Alex several decent offers to sell me that bookstore. The place was bleeding him dry. But no. He had to be stubborn. The town needed a bookstore. Who ever heard of such nonsense?" Roger wiped his forehead with the back of his hand. "Now, I'm prepared to make a fair offer. A pawnshop in the middle of town is just what Fair Haven needs."

Maggie squinted at Roger as if he'd just said, "An epidemic of lice is just what Fair haven needs." "I'm not through with all the paperwork, Roger. And you will probably have to deal with his son, Joshua, for any sales or…"

"Is he here?" Roger barked.

"Is who here?" Maggie snapped right back in her usual annoyed and frustrated tone.

"Joshua, his son." Roger looked at Maggie and shrugged.

"If he is, I wouldn't know. I've never met him," Maggie said, happy to be of no real help to Roger Hawes.

He shook his head and looked around for a moment and then looked down at Maggie. "Where's the kitchen? Do you have coffee?" he asked with his lips pulled down like a bull-dog's jowls.

Maggie pointed to a hallway on her left but didn't utter another word as she watched him slip away to drink the free coffee and orange juice and probably gobble down half the pastries she'd brought. Mr. Whitfield had always liked the pastries from Tammy McCarthy's Bakery, which was just a block down from the bookstore. Actually, she was pretty sure it was Tammy he liked. She was a pistol with bright-red hair and false eyelashes. She'd paid her respects earlier when she'd brought over more than the two boxes of almond croissants Maggie had ordered.

"He was such a good man, Maggie. And he thought so highly of you," Tammy had said before dabbing the corners of her eyes with a lacy kerchief.

"Thank you, Tammy," Maggie replied, biting her tongue so as not to cry.

*Hopefully, the other mourners had enough of an appetite to eat all the almond croissants already*, Maggie thought, and she was sure Mr. Whitfield would have agreed with her. She would never forget how Roger would come to the bookstore and look up and down the shelves as he spoke to Mr. Whitfield.

"You're not getting any younger. What are you going to do with this place? When was the last time you turned a profit?"

he'd say as he looked at the books as if they had tentacles or were covered in spiderwebs.

Maggie had never said anything, but had it been her bookstore, she would have told him to get out. And if he'd ever set foot inside her store again, making such vulgar comments, she'd have him thrown in the hoosegow.

The wake was scheduled to go from eleven in the morning until six in the evening. Maggie had brought a book, hoping that she could just sit quietly with Mr. Whitfield and read like she'd done with him at the store. But it was as if they were giving away free cemetery plots, and a steady flux of people kept coming and going. Maggie was sure these people stayed longer at Mr. Whitfield's wake than they ever had in his store. Plus, it was still raining outside. Maggie knew she should have been grateful that the folks came even in the bad weather, but it annoyed her. By the time Joshua Whitfield arrived, Maggie was in a fouler mood than usual.

## Chapter 3

An unfamiliar face appeared in the viewing room behind Mr. and Mrs. Calvin Toonsley. The latter were the elite of Fair Haven, and although Maggie couldn't recall the last time either one of them had come into the bookstore, she was not surprised they'd shown up. Anywhere they could be seen was the place they were going to be. Mrs. Toonsley wore an appropriate black dress that hugged her perfect figure, with gold fixtures dangling from each finger and wrist. Mr. Toonsley was in a similarly sharp black suit and tie. But the man behind them was a stranger. A very handsome stranger.

Maggie tugged at the sleeves of her sweater and smoothed out her skirt as the young man approached. He had a clean-cut style about him and wore black pants and a gray sweater. His hair had gotten wet from the rain, and so had his cheeks. At least that was what Maggie thought until he came closer and she realized he was crying. He walked over to the casket and knelt on the kneeler. He was there for a while, and no one bothered him. Finally, after wiping his eyes and blinking back any more tears, he turned and walked over to Maggie.

"Are you Margaret Bell?" he asked with a weak smile.

A Book to Kill For

"I am," Maggie replied, her face twisting like it usually did. Why would a handsome guy like this be coming up to her? He must want something.

"I'm Joshua Whitfield. Alexander was my dad. He told me all about you."

"Oh. I'm sorry, he barely mentioned you to me," Maggie blurted. "I mean, I'm sorry for your loss. He was a wonderful man."

"That's what everyone keeps telling me. It's nice that he was so well tended to," Joshua said as he looked over Maggie's face.

She swallowed hard and tried to think of something to say, but nothing coherent or even halfway logical was forming in her head. Mr. Whitfield had never mentioned how handsome his son was. Truthfully, he'd only mentioned his son once or twice, and that had been to complain about Joshua's choice of wife. Maggie decided not to ask about it.

"I'm sorry. There are a few people I need to talk to. Do you know where the funeral director is? I've got to square away the bill and a few other things," Joshua said.

"Uhm, he should be in his office." Maggie pointed to the hallway toward the kitchen. There was an office back there, too.

"Thanks, Margaret. I'd really like to chat with you again when all this is finished," he said as he took her hand in his to shake.

"Really?" Maggie asked before pushing up her glasses with her other hand.

"Yeah. Since I'll be renovating the bookstore, I'll need to know what can go," he said with a sad smile.

"Renovating the bookstore? What for?" Maggie came to life as if she'd received an electric shock.

"I know my father. He'd been using his pension to pay for the place. It wasn't making any money," Joshua replied. "I've got to do something with it."

"Well, your father loved that bookstore exactly the way it is. It was more than just about making money. There are beautiful books there. Books you can't find anywhere else. The kind of books people don't even write anymore," Maggie huffed. "And you want to come and change it all? You want to know what can go? Well, none of it. That's what can go."

Joshua looked at Maggie. For a moment, she got caught up in his eyes, which were the same strange hazel color as his father's. But they twinkled as if he had a secret. Then a smile crept across his lips, making him even more handsome. Maggie didn't like it one bit.

"My dad told me you'd react this way. Look, now isn't the time to talk. But I look forward to working with you," Joshua replied before turning and walking toward the funeral director's office.

"Working with me?" she muttered. She looked down at Mr. Whitfield, who she could have sworn was smirking at her. "Alexander Whitfield, what have you done?"

———

Joshua Whitfield stood at the funeral director's door, waiting for him to get off the phone. The man wore an elegant pinstriped suit and pinky ring and spoke calmly and quietly to whoever was on the other end of the line. Religious pictures and prayers hung on the walls. The neatly organized desk, a hulking oak monstrosity with intricate carvings around the top and the base, took up almost the entire room. There were a coffee pot and a tray of bread and cheese especially for him in the corner. He put one finger up the second he saw Joshua, who nodded in response.

Joshua didn't mind a few seconds of not speaking to anyone. He looked toward the room that held his father and watched Margaret Bell. Alexander had spoken about her dozens of times, but never had he mentioned how pretty she was. Not like that Samantha what's-her-name who had walked into the funeral home at the same time Joshua had. She was sexy and knew it, and Joshua was pretty sure that most of this quaint little town did too. But Margaret was different. Of course, according to his dad, Margaret was really smart, had a dry sense of humor, and was painfully shy. That Joshua could see as she stood close by his dad's casket the way a small child might cling to her mother's leg.

But there was something more than cute about her. It was probably very inappropriate to think about such things at his dad's wake. But Joshua thought his dad had kept her looks a secret from him just so he could look down from heaven at this exact moment and laugh.

"Mr. Whitfield." The funeral director snapped him out of his thoughts.

"Yes. I'm sorry." Joshua gave Maggie one last look before focusing on the task at hand.

"My name is Dennis Lorenz. I'm very sorry for your loss." The funeral director stood from his desk and barely reached a height of five-six. Funny, Joshua thought he had looked a lot more imposing while he was sitting.

"Thank you," Joshua said. "I just got into town and wanted to know what expenses needed to be wrapped up."

"No expenses. Your father had everything paid for beforehand," Dennis replied.

"What? How could that be? He didn't have any money," Joshua said.

"He made all the arrangements more than two years ago. I handled all of the details personally. He didn't want a big fuss. Mostly, he just wanted to have a quiet affair. Frankly, from the way he talked, I'm pleasantly surprised at the outpouring of sympathy from our little town." Dennis smiled. He was handsome, even if he was short, and looked like a character out of a movie from the forties.

"I just don't get this. I know my dad's pension was almost

completely gone. The bookstore didn't make any money. Where did he get the funds for this?"

Joshua was frustrated. He knew he shouldn't be and should just be thankful, but he wasn't. He'd been gone for several years, trying to make his marriage work. When that had failed, he had been embarrassed to face his dad. Not that Alexander had ever given him a reason to feel that way. But like so many kids, it didn't matter how old he got; he wanted his dad to be proud of him. And how could Joshua make his father proud when he couldn't make himself proud?

"Obviously, this is making you upset. I'd promised I wouldn't tell anyone," Dennis said and walked over to a bookcase that was loaded with important-looking books. He pulled down an especially old copy of a book titled *Smoke from the Altar* by Louis L'Amour.

"What is this?" Joshua asked.

"Your father's payment. I love western novels. This book is a first edition, and we sort of made a trade. I know it isn't what you expected, but your father was not what most people expected. He was the last of the great thinkers, a real gentleman," Dennis said.

"He paid you with a book?" Joshua smirked.

"He did indeed. And I assure you that everything he requested has been carried out to perfection. Tammy's Bakery provided the food in the kitchen. The casket was lined with powder-blue satin. Of course, he has an American flag for his time in Korea," Dennis assured Joshua.

"It certainly sounds like he handled everything."

"You can be sure of that. Again, I'm sorry for your loss." Dennis shook Joshua's hand again.

When Joshua stepped out of the office, he didn't know what to think about what his dad had done. He couldn't be mad at him. His dad had paid for what he wanted in his own way. The man would never take a handout, so he gave away what he had.

When Joshua looked toward the viewing room, he saw his father's pretty assistant again. He wanted to go talk to her a little more, but she was obviously well known in town. She probably had a boyfriend or maybe two.

———

MAGGIE'S THOUGHTS were all jumbled as she worried about her job. She hated Joshua Whitfield for it. And she couldn't help but think that he was absolutely dreamy, and she'd decided she hated him for that too. As she watched him walk toward the funeral director's office, her face contorted as if she'd smelled something bad.

Mr. Whitfield had paid for his funeral with a first edition of one of his books. Maggie was convinced that Mr. Lorenz had skimped on what her previous boss had wanted. He had prayer cards of St. Anthony and donations to the library in lieu of flowers. But Maggie had not been told where his ashes were supposed to go. She expected them to stay in the bookstore. But since she wasn't family, even though everyone in town knew she'd worked at the bookstore for six years, she had no say in anything. It left a bitter taste in her mouth.

And as if that wasn't bad enough, Maggie found herself walking back and forth just a few steps and looking at Mr. Whitfield, the nicest man she'd ever known, and hoping that maybe he wasn't really dead. Maybe he'd wink at her and confess that he was playing some grand game on the whole town. But of course, he wasn't. Instead, he was playing a cruel game on her by not mentioning how handsome his son was and then having him just show up out of the blue. Joshua Whitfield, who was going to talk to her about her job and tell her what they were going to do differently, even though Maggie had been handling all the gory details for years. She knew where every book was, how much each cost, and how much certain books were worth and had read almost half the inventory. She felt a certain stake in the company even if she wasn't a blood relative. It made her purse her lips and twist them to the side.

"I know that feeling," Calvin Toonsley chuckled as he snuck up on Maggie.

"What? Oh. Sorry, Mr. Toonsley. Thank you for coming," Maggie said as she adjusted her glasses again. She'd only spoken to Mr. Toonsley on a couple of occasions, but the man was hard to forget. He mentioned his profession a dozen times per sentence and would often check his genuine Rolex just as many times in front of whoever he was talking to.

"It's a shame the old man had to go. But I guess we'll all have to go sometime, right, Maggie? That was a nice little shop he had. Although I've never been much of a reader, except for the stock market, right?" He grinned.

Maggie forced an awkward smile. "Well, Mr. Whitfield enjoyed any visitors who came to the store. He wasn't worried about whether anyone bought anything."

"That's probably why he was barely staying afloat." Calvin Toonsley cleared his throat. "I tried to tell him to invest. You know, the stock market is my business."

"So I've heard," Maggie replied.

Mrs. Samantha Toonsley was on the other side of the room, chatting with some of the women from town. She gabbed with a smile on her face as if she was at some kind of charity event, trying to raise money.

"I understand collecting, but I'd rather collect on my investments than on some old books. Know what I mean?" Calvin asked with a wink. "If you have a couple thousand dollars, Maggie, I'd be happy to help you make a couple of strategic investments. That is what I do, after all. I can't guarantee you'll end up as comfortable as Mrs. Toonsley and me, but you might have a couple extra dollars in the bank. After you sell the bookstore, just come and see me, and we'll talk."

"Who told you I was selling the bookstore?" Maggie snapped.

"No one. I just assumed," Calvin replied with a shrug.

"Yeah, well, no one is selling anything. I don't have a couple thousand dollars, Calvin," Maggie snapped and handed him back his card.

"You sound like my son, Heath. Home from college for a couple weeks and thinks the world owes him a living," Calvin huffed. "He's been this way every time he comes home, whether it was boarding school or now Harvard. I don't know what it is with you young people and always doing everything the hard way."

"I graduated college over a decade ago, Calvin," Maggie said.

"Oh, uh, I thought you were younger than...well, I see. So...you probably should call me sometime, to talk about your financial future. Even if you don't sell the bookstore," Calvin stuttered.

When he didn't get a response from Maggie, who stared at him with wide, dry brown eyes as if he was slowly turning colors, Calvin cleared his throat, tapped on the edge of Mr. Whitfield's coffin, and walked toward the kitchen.

Maggie took a deep breath, but before she could even exhale, Mrs. Toonsley was at her side. The smile she'd been showcasing to the others had been replaced by a droopy, overly sympathetic expression.

"You poor dear," she said and pulled Maggie in for a tight embrace. The smell of her perfume stung Maggie's eyes and made her blink. It was like a heavy quilt that had marinated in dry cinnamon for a couple years.

"Thanks, Samantha," Maggie grunted as the air was squeezed out of her.

"Walter was such a wonderful man," Samantha said as she pulled back and touched the edge of the coffin.

"Who?" Maggie huffed.

"Walter." Samantha looked at Maggie and then the coffin and back at Maggie again.

"His name is Alexander."

Maggie squinted and wrinkled her nose. There were still several hours of this wake to go, and she was exhausted. If only she could have traded places with Mr. Whitfield, at least until everyone left.

"Of course it is. Of course it is. I knew that. I even bought a couple of books from him." Samantha was an expert at recovering from an awkward situation.

"I remember. You bought a fourth edition of *Lancaster Boots* and a regular copy of *To Kill a Mockingbird*. How did you like the books?" Maggie replied with a slight smile.

"I didn't read them. *Lancaster Boots* was an investment. I saw that was going for over a thousand dollars on eBay. Calvin isn't the only one who knows what things are worth. And my son needed *To Kill a Mockingbird* for school. Did you hear what I just said? My son needed to kill a mockingbird for school. What kind of school is that?" She chortled at her own joke.

Maggie smiled politely and nodded before wrinkling her nose with annoyance. "I read that when I was in eighth grade," Maggie replied.

"Yes, well, you're bookish like that. My son, he's…more outgoing, you know. He's very popular at Harvard. He belongs to Phi Beta Kappa, same as his father," Samantha replied proudly. "He's in town for a visit. Now, if I could just get him married off. Are you seeing anyone?" She chortled.

"Not at the moment." Maggie shook her head.

"Oh, honey, I was only joking. You aren't Heath's type. He goes for the more outgoing kind of girls. You're just a little too…uh…er…"

"Bookish?" Maggie tugged at her sleeves again.

Samantha cleared her throat and once again tilted her head to the right and frowned in annoyance rather than out of real sympathy.

"I had spoken to Walt...Alexander about purchasing another book. *Sierra Madre Heights?* I believe he said he had a first edition. Do you know anything about that? If it would still be possible for me to purchase it?" She eyeballed Maggie as if looking for a chink in her armor.

"I can't say anything about that. It doesn't belong to me. It all belongs to his son now. Heaven only knows what he plans to do," Maggie mumbled.

"Is he getting rid of the older books in the bookstore? Are you selling them too?" Samantha asked, her eyes narrowing as she watched Maggie. "I mean, they are just old books collecting dust. If no one has bought them by now, I doubt anyone will."

"I'm meeting with his son to discuss my job. I'm sure he'll say what he's doing with the inventory," Maggie replied. "He came in with you and your husband. I thought you were talking to him."

"Oh, is that that handsome young man who came in before us? My goodness." Samantha flipped her blond hair over her shoulder and looked around for Joshua.

Maggie rolled her eyes again then looked at Alexander and wondered why he hadn't talked to her about this day. They had both known it was coming. But why hadn't he prepared her? Why hadn't he suggested a book to help her cope or given her some kind of sage advice like he was always doing and she was always ignoring? Why hadn't he reminded her that he was old and not going to be around forever?

"Oh, I think the mayor just walked in. If you'll excuse me," Samantha said. She barely finished the sentence before walking away to slip her manicured fingernails through the mayor's arm and hold on tight. Sadly, the mayor looked all too happy to see her.

Maggie looked around at all the people. She liked the book ladies who often visited and bought some of the second-hand titles Mr. Whitfield carried. There were a couple of boys from the high school who had regularly come in to trade their old copies of the *Dune Chronicles* for a couple dollars or to swap out for some old pulp sci-fi.

But other than that, she wasn't sure what all these people were doing here. They never came into the store, let alone bought anything. All Maggie could think was that they were bored and had nothing else to do.

It had started to rain on the day Mr. Whitfield had died and had continued on and off until today.

"I heard the forecast say it's supposed to continue raining for the next week," one of the mourners said in passing, giving Maggie a sad grin as she slowly glided along. "You can bet the bridges will be closed."

Maggie didn't care if the bridges closed. There was no need for her to go anywhere outside of town. Everything she needed was right here. She looked at Mr. Whitfield and felt the sting of tears but quickly blinked them back. There were just too many people around.

Slowly, the room began to empty as people paid their respects for a few polite moments then went about their business. They ran to their cars, jackets and purses held over their heads as the rain continued to fall.

She hadn't noticed until she was almost completely alone that her feet were aching. She'd stood next to Mr. Whitfield for hours. It wasn't that she thought he needed protecting but more that she felt safer beside him. The thought that he was no longer going to be there for her to talk to and joke with seeped into her heart like a slow leak in a tire.

Without worrying about looking inappropriate, Maggie pulled her book out of her purse. *The Streets of Laredo.* She opened it to the first page, but her vision instantly blurred as her eyes flooded with tears. She didn't want to cry. She hadn't cried when the paramedics came or when they told her Mr. Whitfield had died quickly and probably hadn't even known it happened. "*He didn't suffer at all,*" the paramedics had told her.

For that she was grateful. But part of her was mad at him. He was the closest thing to family she had. And now he was gone. What was she going to do?

"Maggie?" Tammy was the only other person who had been at the wake for its entirety. "Honey, are you all right?"

Maggie opened her mouth to speak, but nothing came out. All she could do was shake her head no. Tammy, who smelled like cinnamon and sugar, hurried to Maggie's side, sat down next to her, and put her arm around her. They sat there for a few minutes before the wake was officially over. Then they said their good-byes and left the Pearlman Funeral Home.

But Maggie's night wasn't over yet.

## Chapter 4

"I'll be okay," Maggie insisted as she walked with Tammy, who was going to her car.

"I can give you a ride home. It's no problem," Tammy offered.

"No. I feel like walking. Really, thanks, Tammy. I'll stop by and see you next week," Maggie replied and pulled away from the woman in order to get a few steps ahead of her.

"Do that, honey." Tammy waved before getting into her car and speeding away.

The rain had let up, and when Maggie looked up, she could see a couple of stars peeking through the clouds that were swiftly sailing overhead. Where had the day gone? Even though her feet had been killing her inside the funeral home, she did feel like walking. Truthfully, she wanted to stop at the bookstore. Poe was there and was probably wondering where his food was.

Mr. Whitfield had lived in the apartment above the bookstore. A simple set of creaky stairs at the back of the store led to his flat, the door of which was never locked. Maggie had been in his apartment enough times to know where the cat food was.

After pulling her key from the chain around her neck, Maggie unlocked the deadbolt on the store's front door and then slipped the key into the doorknob. After the familiar click-click, she pushed the door open. Tiny windchimes welcomed her back. As soon as she stepped through the door, the smell of parchment filled her nose. But the space was eerily quiet. The sound of soft music or the television coming from upstairs was not there. The light from the stairway was off. Only the light from the streetlamp gave Maggie anything to see by. She snapped the deadbolt back into place.

Maggie knew the store like the back of her hand. She knew it so well that even in the dark, she knew to step over the stack of books on the floor by the counter and wove around the coffee-table books that stuck out from the fourth bookshelf in the third row.

She snapped on the old-fashioned light that had a base in the shape of a pineapple, and suddenly, everything was familiar again. She looked around and felt funny at the fact that everything was just as she'd left it. Everything was the same but different. A world of different.

As she walked to the back of the store, she flipped on the lights to the stairs. The creaks were all familiar and comforting in a strange way. Once at the landing, she gave the doorknob a twist. The door opened easily. With just a few seconds of fumbling, she found the light switch, snapped it on, and stepped into the late Alexander Whitfield's apartment.

It was simply decorated with books, books, and more books. There were oriental area rugs on the floor. A high-backed leather chair sat in the corner next to a round table with Mr. Whitfield's coffee cup still sitting on it.

Poe, who seemed to spend most of his life on a windowsill either in the apartment or in the bookshop, was lazily stretched out on the davenport across from the leather chair and next to the old-fashioned Victrola, which still worked.

"Boy, have you got it rough," Maggie said as she scooped

the cat into her arms. "What am I going to do with you? From the sound of things, I think we are both out on our ear if Joshua Whitfield has any say in it."

Maggie walked to the kitchenette, put the cat down on the floor, and checked his food bowl. He had plenty of dry food left. She added fresh water to his drinking dish and scraped the second half of a can of cat food into a third bowl, but Poe had no interest in it.

"I'm not all that hungry either," Maggie admitted.

Just then, she heard a strange sound coming from the bookstore. At first, she thought it was just her imagination. But when she saw Poe's ears perk up as the animal looked toward the open apartment door, she knew she'd heard something.

"I am not in the mood for any games," she huffed. With all her frustration and anger at the unfairness of the situation, Maggie went stomping across the floor and down the stairs into the bookstore, muttering many unladylike things along the way. Once she got to the main floor, she shouted.

"The bookstore is closed. See the sign?" She pointed to a dark figure in a hoodie standing at the door. There was no way she could see his face. He stared at her from the black oval where his face should be.

"Come back in the morning, please. We open at nine!"

The man's desire for a late-night book would have to be satisfied another way. He hesitated for a second then nodded, waved, and walked away.

Maggie's first thought was that the man was probably drunk. She found it a little spooky, but in taking a couple of self-defense classes in college, she had learned that noise was the enemy of an attacker. And if they weren't an attacker, the feeling of unease around Maggie's nosiness was enough to get them to quickly walk away. As had been the desired result just now. And if that failed and she was confronted by an assailant, her job would be to swing and kick and bite and scream all at once until she either beat them back or passed out from exhaustion.

After going back upstairs, Maggie decided she was too tired to go home. Her fear was that this place wasn't going to be around too much longer, so she was going to enjoy it for as long as she could. She shut and locked the apartment door, put on the teapot, and slipped out of her skirt and sweater.

Mr. Whitfield had an electric fireplace that slowly spun an orange kaleidoscope between two fake logs to simulate crackling embers, throwing warm colors all over the room as it generated a steady heat. Next to it were an iron poker, shovel, and broom. It just struck her now that those utensils were not really necessary, but they made the fireplace seem that much more authentic. It was rather lovely. Maggie poured herself a cup of hot tea, stretched out on the davenport in her slip and bare feet, and pulled a soft flannel blanket over her legs. The memories of all the stories Mr. Whitfield had told her about his life came back a little at a time. She sipped her tea as tears filled her eyes, and she thought how tragic it would be when someone else took over this little apartment. She cringed at the thought of some younger person with a futon to sit and sleep on and milk crates as functioning pieces of furniture.

"You have an older person's sense of style, Mags. How did you get that?" Mr. Whitfield had once said to her when she came to work wearing a vintage beaded sweater that had been popular in the 1950s.

"I don't know. I guess I just like what's considered old-fashioned," Maggie replied. "I guess that explains why I like you."

She remembered making a lot of comments like that and Mr. Whitfield laughing at every one of them. She wiped her eyes and leaned back against the soft throw pillow. The fireplace mechanism was soothing. Soon Maggie felt her eyelids drooping. It had been a long day, and she still had paperwork and personal items to gather. And then there was the bad news destined to come from Joshua Whitfield tomorrow.

"No. I'm not going to think about that now. I'll think about that tomorrow, said Scarlett O'Hara," she muttered as her lids got heavier.

Poe slunk along the floor, stopping by the door to do a little quick grooming before bed.

Maggie wasn't sure how long she had been asleep, but she was sure the sound of the door closing downstairs woke her up. The room was still gold and orange from the fireplace rotating its artificial fire. She held her breath and strained to hear over the whirring mechanism. Just as she was about to relax her body, an all-too-familiar sound rushed to her ears like a squirrel might dash across the street: the floorboards downstairs creaked.

No. No one could have gotten in. They would have had to break the glass door, and that would have made a ton of noise.

"You're just hearing things. Dreaming," she said, her own hushed voice cutting like a gong through the quiet apartment.

As her muscles started to relax, she noticed Poe sitting on the oriental carpet in front of the door. He was staring at it, his tail lazily waving back and forth. Maggie's first thought was that the little animal was waiting for his master to come home. Her heart ached for the cat until it froze solid in her chest. Someone or something had kicked over the stack of books on the floor by the desk downstairs. It was unmistakable.

Why would anyone break into the bookstore? They had to know there was no money in the register. But then she remembered the hooded person jiggling the front door handle. Had he come back? Had she slept through him breaking the glass door or jimmying the back door? Maggie threw the blanket aside and sat up. She leaned toward the door, not daring to get up and give away her own position by stepping on a loose board.

Then, as if the intruder had set off another alarm, Maggie heard someone knock into the coffee-table books that stuck out of the bookshelf. Mr. Whitfield, no matter how long those books had been there, had always managed to bump into them.

When Maggie heard the gruff grunt of a male voice, she stood up. Was it? Could it be? Poe was still sitting in front of the door as if he was expecting Mr. Whitfield to come through it. Maggie swallowed hard, but her mouth had gone dry. The sound of footsteps coming up the stairs to the apartment sent a rush of adrenaline through her veins. Sweat covered her forehead and the back of her neck.

"Mr. Whitfield?" she called.

It would be just like that devious old man to come back as a ghost to taunt and tease her from the grave. In her heart, she didn't think it was a ghost, but when the footfalls stopped at the mention of his name, Maggie began to tremble.

Poe's tail was the only thing expressing any concern as it began to whip back and forth with excitement. Animals were keener when it came to paranormal entities, or at least that was what Maggie had read somewhere. The feline didn't seem to be upset. But then again, he was used to the occasional person coming and going. What would he care if a violent intruder was coming in to rob Mr. Whitfield's apartment?

Before she could take a deep breath, Maggie heard the steps start again, and they had not changed direction. They advanced on the door. Before she could get to the kitchenette to pull a knife from the butcher block, the sound of keys in the lock pushed Maggie into action. She stretched across the small parlor, grabbed the coffee cup, and just as the lock snapped and the door opened, she let the thing fly. It crashed into the doorframe, shattering into a million pieces. Poe ran into the bathroom.

"What the heck!" the man shouted.

"Don't come any closer!" Maggie grabbed the shovel from the side of the fireplace and raised it over her head. "If I'm going down, you're coming with me!"

"Margaret?" Joshua Whitfield stood in the doorway with shards of the shattered coffee cup around his feet.

"Joshua? What are you doing here?" Maggie snapped.

"This is my dad's home. What are you doing here?" he shouted before the vision of Maggie in a slip distracted him. He never would have guessed such a cute little figure lurked underneath her buttoned-up sweater and wide skirt.

"I didn't feel like going all the way home," Maggie replied, putting her hand on her hip before realizing she was just in her slip. With a squeak of embarrassment, she grabbed the flannel blanket and wrapped it around herself.

"Did you stay at my dad's place often?" Joshua asked with a look of horror.

"Bite your tongue. Your father was as dear to me as my own father. I hope he haunts you for making a comment like that," she scolded.

They stood there for a few seconds before Maggie started toward the kitchenette to get the broom and dustpan.

"Wait! Don't move!" Joshua shouted. "You don't have any shoes on. Let me do that."

"I'm fully capable of sweeping a floor," Maggie huffed as she grabbed the tools from the small utility closet in the corner.

"Good to know. I may have a use for you yet," Joshua replied before yanking the broom and pan from her. "Now stay put until I get this all swept up."

"You need a flashlight if you are going to get every piece," Maggie instructed.

"Can you just be quiet for a moment? I think I know how to sweep up a broken mug. Sheesh. My father said you were this polite, shy young lady. You don't seem all that shy to me." He looked at her face and then down at her bare feet.

"Very funny. Your wife must be in stitches all the time with such a witty husband," Maggie replied.

"My *ex*-wife will tell you I had a very good sense of humor, thank you very much," Joshua replied as he continued sweeping.

Maggie stopped. She wrinkled up her face; she didn't want to continue this game. Mr. Whitfield had said that his son was married, but he had never spoken of his daughter-in-law in any way—good, bad, or indifferent. He had only spoken about his son and beamed with pride every time he did. Maggie swallowed.

"I'm sorry. I didn't know," she said. She adjusted her blanket around her body, making sure none of the skin on her shoulders, arms, or neck showed.

"It's all right. My dad didn't know either. I didn't tell him. He never liked my wife," Joshua said.

Just as he finished sweeping, Poe came out of his hiding place and, with reckless abandon, rubbed his entire body along Joshua's right leg then continued the display over his left.

"Well, that's really none of my business," Maggie said and tiptoed over to the couch, where her clothes lay on the floor. She picked them up and went into the bathroom, shutting the door behind her and hooking the little latch into place.

Within a few minutes, she emerged fully dressed except for her feet, which were still bare.

"Do you want to stay for a cup of coffee or something?" Joshua asked as he watched her scurry around the small apartment, picking up her stockings and shoes.

"No," she replied without explanation. Of course, she would have loved to stay and chat and get to know Joshua. It was amazing that he appeared to be even more handsome now than he had been before.

"Look, Margaret, I'm going to need your help with the shop. Getting everything in order and..." Joshua began.

"I'll help you out of respect for your father. But the fact that you can just close up his shop, get rid of all his books and the things he held dear, well, I guess the apple fell far from the tree," Maggie replied. She was tired and heartbroken.

"My father didn't know how to run a business, and I…"

"I'm sorry for your loss, Joshua. The world is a little grayer without your father around," Maggie said. She stomped to the door, yanked it open, and slammed it shut behind her then hurried downstairs.

Like an experienced cat burglar, she maneuvered around the spilled books, unlocked the door, stepped out into the cool night, and took a deep breath. More rain was on the way. She could smell it.

She went back to Pearlman Funeral Home, where her car was waiting. In no time, she was at her own home. Her heart was still broken that she would not see Mr. Whitfield tomorrow. Instead, she'd see his handsome son, who was nothing like him.

## Chapter 5

**M**aggie wasn't sure if the sound she'd heard was in her dream or in reality. She heard the knock on her door again. With her eyes barely open, she got up from her bed, grabbed her fuzzy, warm robe, and pulled it around her shoulders as she walked to the front door. She could see through the lace curtains across her door that it was her landlady, Vivian Peacock. There was no such thing as a quick conversation with Widow Peacock.

"Good morning, Mrs. Peacock," Maggie grumbled. "Is everything okay?"

"I was about to ask you the same thing. I saw you got home very late last night, and I know, with the passing of Mr. Whitfield, that you are probably just drowning in a sea of despair."

Mrs. Peacock was also in her robe, which zipped modestly up to her neck. She owned a very large house and rented her guest house, all one thousand square feet of it, to Maggie at a more than reasonable price. The only catch was that Mrs. Peacock did like to talk—a lot—about anyone and everyone in Fair Haven.

"I'm not drowning. Not yet, anyway," Maggie muttered and managed a smile.

"Well, I must ask if you've decided what you'll be doing for a paycheck now that the bookstore is going to be closed." Mrs. Peacock rubbed the back of her neck. The only thing she liked more than gossip was collecting the rent.

"What? Who told you it was being closed?" Maggie was suddenly wide awake as if she'd just gotten a shot of caffeine injected directly into her heart.

"Well, I just assumed, since Mr. Whitfield's son hired my carpenter, Bo Logan, to tear the inside of it down and that he had decided to sell it to Roger Hawes to be turned into a pawnshop," Mrs. Peacock said, her eyes narrowing. "Have you heard something different?"

"I haven't heard anything. But that's because I'm the last to know everything," Maggie huffed. "If you'll excuse me, Mrs. Peacock, I have to get to the bookshop."

"Well, let me know what's happening so I know I'll be able to count on rent. I am on a fixed income, you know," Mrs. Peacock replied.

If Maggie had had a nickel for every time she'd heard Mrs. Peacock say she was on a fixed income, she'd have been able to rent the big house for more than a year.

"Yeah, Mrs. Peacock. I'll do that. I'm sorry, I have to get to work." Maggie smiled and shut the door as Mrs. Peacock stepped off the tiny porch and walked toward the big house in fuzzy slippers that click-clacked along the sidewalk.

Without wasting any time, Maggie jumped into the shower, washed, and dressed in her most sensible black slacks and a pink cardigan. Before she hurried out the door, she dabbed on a little of the perfume she usually saved for special occasions and quickly snapped on a vintage pearl pin that she'd found at a thrift store for a few dollars. She had no time to do her hair and quickly piled it on top of her head in a tight bun.

As she hurried to her car, she saw the sky was the same dreary gray it had been for the past few days. It matched her mood.

Without a drop of coffee or anything in her stomach, she sped to the bookshop. She gasped when she saw the front door wide open, with men with tool belts and bulky boots carrying planks of wood inside. She parked the car almost up on the curb and marched into the place as if she was going to war.

"Margaret, I'm glad you're here," Joshua said as soon as he saw her walk in.

A fresh hole had been knocked in the wall that, for years, had separated the bookshop from the empty furniture store-front next door.

"What are you doing? Don't you realize that some of these books are valuable? All this dust and dirt…or are you just planning on throwing them all away?" Maggie demanded without preamble.

"Well, good morning to you," Joshua said.

"Am I fired?" Maggie asked.

"What?"

"Am I fired? Or are you just going to torture me until I quit so you don't have to pay unemployment?" Maggie snapped.

"No, you aren't fired. But if you want to quit then quit," Joshua replied.

"Of course I don't want to quit. I loved this job and the bookstore. But you've just come busting in here like a tornado, and it looks like…you've made a real mess of things."

Maggie's voice and temper lowered when she looked into Joshua's face. She didn't dare look anywhere else, as he was absolutely delicious in his tool belt and jeans. She shook her head to dispel the image and instead looked into his hazel eyes. She felt the tension leave her face and quickly turned to examine the big hole in the wall.

"I'm not getting rid of the bookstore," Joshua said.

"You're not? I can still work here?" Maggie blurted without thinking.

"Yeah," Joshua said with a smile. "I don't really like to read."

She recoiled as if Joshua had just revealed he had a touch of Ebola. Didn't like to read? How could he be Alexander Whitfield's son and not like to read?

"You don't?" Again, the words just fell out.

"No. I'd rather watch a movie." He chuckled.

Maggie squared her shoulders as if she were getting ready to slap Joshua across the face for saying something so offensive.

"But I know that a bookstore can be a good business if you know how to run it. My dad, God bless him, had good intentions. But he wasn't a good businessman."

"Your father was an extremely intelligent man. He kept this place open, and there wasn't a book on the planet he hadn't heard of. Why, I wouldn't be surprised if the Library of Congress could learn a thing or two from him. And his knowledge of old books was…" Maggie defended her old boss but stopped speaking when Joshua put up his hand.

"Yes, he knew a lot about old books. But he didn't know how to sell them. And if he did, for one reason or another, he wouldn't. It was almost like he didn't want to make any money." Joshua shook his head. "Well, that is why I need your help. I need you to help me rearrange the bookstore so we can bring in some new inventory."

"What?"

"Yeah, we need to get some of the popular stuff in the windows to attract more customers." Joshua smiled.

"Popular stuff?" Maggie's stomach twisted. "To get more customers?"

"Yeah, you know, like that series with the vampire teenagers or that one with the weirdo lawyer who has a dungeon in his house and his secretary likes it. You know what I'm talking about?" Joshua nodded.

"Yeah, you're talking about filling your dad's store with garbage," Maggie blurted then swallowed hard.

"It might be garbage, but it's what people want to read. I'm not here to defend or deny them their poison. I'm just going to put it out there, and hopefully they'll get it from us instead of Amazon." Joshua smiled. "And once we get all the new inventory, people can enjoy a hot cup of coffee or tea next door. Or, if they'd prefer to come at night, wine or beer after five."

"You're kidding," Maggie huffed.

"No. That's what I'm doing. Bo, that big guy over there, he's got the blueprints, and we should have the whole place completed in less than two weeks." Joshua clicked his tongue and winked at Maggie as he pointed to a man who looked like a bear in a flannel shirt. He waved to Maggie, but she quickly looked away, her cheeks blazing.

"If people want coffee, they can just go to Tammy's Bakery down the street," Maggie said, hoping to discourage Joshua's plans. But the twinkle in his eyes told her she was too late.

"Aha. See, I already made a deal with her that I'd sell her pastries here if she would be willing to make me a few exclusives just for the coffee shop." Joshua rocked on his heels.

"When do I have to order these stupid trendy books? And what about your father's library?" Maggie was sure she was going to either cry or throw up.

"There will be room for both. But the old stuff will go in the back. I want at least the front half of the store filled with the new stuff. I'll have a list for you by tomorrow. Today, maybe you could start moving some of the books to the back shelves. Get rid of anything that you don't think is worth keeping," Joshua said.

He went to talk to Bo. She stood there with her mouth open.

*Get rid of anything that you don't think is worth keeping.* The words echoed in her head as if he'd just told her there was a nest of wasps he expected her to stick her hand in. As long as she was in charge of this task, there wouldn't be a single book thrown away. She'd find a place for everything, even if she had to hide some of them to save them from such a fate.

## Chapter 6

A couple of days had gone by, and Maggie had to admit she was enjoying going through all the old books. And true to the promise she had made to herself, not a single book was tossed away. Carefully, she emptied one shelf of books only to reshelve them behind another row. No one would know they were there but her, and that was okay, since she was the only one who would return to read them.

With a pit in her stomach, she placed an order with the distributor Joshua had contacted and ordered the contemporary books he'd requested. In between her tasks, she found herself peeking in Joshua's direction, watching him help hold a stud in place or use a nail gun. Once, she watched as he balanced on top of a ladder and was about to screw something into the ceiling when Bo came charging out of nowhere.

"Whoa! Whoa! Don't touch that!" Bo shouted. "Did you turn the electricity off?"

"Uh, no," Joshua admitted.

"Please, get down off the ladder, Josh." Bo shook his head. "Can you leave the electrical work for us licensed electricians?"

"Just trying to help," Joshua said as he climbed down.

"Yeah, getting electrocuted is not helping," Bo replied and clapped Joshua on the back as soon as his feet were on the ground.

Maggie chuckled a little but then went back to work. She came across a couple of copies of old books she'd never seen before. Their pages were like tracing paper, and they were musty and powdered with dust, making her sneeze.

"Bless you," Joshua called.

Maggie felt butterflies take off inside her chest. What was wrong with her? Mr. Whitfield had said "bless you" every time she sneezed, and she didn't get all goofy inside.

"Thank you," she muttered as she peeked from behind the bookshelf.

Joshua hadn't looked in her direction. He probably didn't even know it was her who'd sneezed. But as she watched him leaning on the new counter next to the new doorway that, just a few days ago, had been nothing more than a hole in the wall, she wondered if he had a girlfriend.

*Where did that thought come from? Maggie, get a hold of yourself,* she thought and shook her head. A guy like him probably had more than one girlfriend. And even if he didn't, he would have no interest in a girl who read.

When the boxes of new books arrived, Maggie stood and stared at them as if they were a gift of fruitcake at Christmastime.

"Are those the books?" Joshua asked.

Maggie was sure he was inquiring just to tease her. He knew how she felt about them. This was just his way of reminding her that he was the boss. And that he was still handsome.

"Yes," she muttered.

"Okay. I was going to get one of the girls from the beauty-supply store down the street to display them in the windows. They've got great displays and…" Joshua started.

"Uh, no," Maggie replied. "It will look nice. I promise."

Joshua looked at Maggie for a minute with a kind smile on his face. "Okay. I just thought you might be too busy clearing away the other titles that…"

"No. If your dad were here, I'd make it look nice for him. I just don't like…never mind." Maggie shook her head.

"Don't like what?"

"I don't like that people will see what I'm doing in the window. I wish it could be more like a surprise." She pushed her glasses up and pinched her lips together.

"I've got an idea." Joshua clomped to the back of the store and upstairs. Within seconds, he returned with three big sheets. "I can tack these across the window for you. A big reveal for the grand opening might be nice."

Maggie almost smiled and said a sincere "thank you" before she caught herself. Instead, she just nodded as he stapled the sheets in place. Part of her would have liked to keep them up permanently. She didn't want anyone looking in or seeing new things then coming in to disturb her and make small talk about the rain that was on its way. The forecast gave the people of Fair Haven one respite from the gray and drizzle. That was today. Starting tonight, rain was predicted for the next week.

"If you need anything else, let me know. I'm going to get back to work," Joshua said.

Maggie just nodded as she looked around the dusty window ledge. The very idea that one of those Barbies from the beauty-supply shop had been about to manhandle these books was enough to make her grind her teeth. They were probably just Joshua's type. How deep could they get when they talked about mascara and lip gloss all day?

First she set to cleaning. Then she scrounged the bookstore for Mr. Whitfield's old trinkets and tables. She moved things around and made a quaint little space, but it needed one more thing: the highbacked leather chair. Quietly, she slipped upstairs. The door was unlocked. With a little maneuvering, she managed to get the chair halfway down the steps before she heard the argument.

"Bo, now isn't the time to talk about this. We have a contract," Joshua said.

"Josh, I told you this was part-time until something came up. My crew has been hired for a real job. I can't tell them I'm turning it down because I am doing a favor for your old man," Bo replied. "The holidays are coming up. We need the money. All my guys do."

"Look, once the place is up and running, I can give you more. But the only reason I hired you in the first place was because you said you'd give me a deal. If I knew you were going to cut and run, I'd have sold the building outright," Joshua replied.

Sell the place outright? Maggie held her breath and listened.

"I'm sorry, Josh. But Roger says he can…"

"Oh, Roger Hawes? I should have known he'd have work for you right about now. The guy hasn't bought or sold anything in six months, but now, because I won't hand over my dad's business, he's going to hire every decent crew in Fair Haven out from under me," Joshua replied.

"Your dealings with Roger are none of my business. All I know is he pays on time and his checks don't bounce. I'm sorry, Josh," Bo said.

"This is not how business is supposed to be done, Bo. You know it. Deep down, you know it. And I won't forget this," Joshua said.

Maggie heard Joshua heading in her direction, so she quickly pretended to struggle with the chair as if she hadn't been listening at all.

"What are you doing?" He chuckled when he saw her.

"I need this for the window," she huffed.

"Well, where am I supposed to sit?"

"There's the davenport," Maggie offered.

"If I don't come home to find someone sleeping on it," he replied before taking the chair from her and carrying it the rest of the way down the stairs.

Maggie didn't let on that she'd heard the conversation between him and Bo. She waited for him to say something, but he didn't. Instead, once he put the chair by the window, he turned around and stomped off upstairs, slamming the door behind him.

Bo and his men were still working when five o'clock rolled around. Joshua had not come down from the upstairs apartment. Maggie decided to hurry home before the rain started. She'd no sooner set foot in her home than a loud crack of thunder ushered in the rain.

"Made it this time," she sighed. She walked over to the thermostat and turned the heat up then flipped on the lights. Her kitchen was a cozy place, with a teakettle always at the ready on the stove. Her evening was quiet, aside from the occasional clap of thunder.

## Chapter 7

That night, Maggie couldn't sleep. Nothing particularly pressing kept her awake. After all, she didn't have anything to worry about if Joshua was going to keep her on in the bookshop. Sure, she'd have to peddle mediocre fiction and nonfiction alike. To her, it was like selling cigarettes to teenagers. But that was part of making a business work. The customer was always right; Mr. Whitfield had said that. Of course, the few customers he'd had were people who appreciated the fine work that went into a first copy of *The Hound of the Baskervilles*. They wouldn't have any desire to read the latest tripe that some big-city paper included on its lists.

"Oh, why am I worrying about it?" she grumbled. She flung the blankets aside and swung her legs off the bed. The clock read 4:59. She was usually up by five thirty anyway. That way, she could read a couple chapters from the books Mr. Whitfield had assigned to her, and they could discuss them throughout the day. She was enjoying *The Streets of Laredo*, but her mind kept drifting. So rather than torture herself this morning, she decided to get up, get dressed, eat something quickly, and just go to work. The window was coming along much better than she'd expected, and having it finished might cheer up Joshua after his argument with Bo.

"Why do you care if he's cheered up?" she muttered to herself as she shuffled to the bathroom.

Maggie's home was decorated in what could only be called secondhand-store chic. It boasted lots of flowers on slipcovers, tablecloths, and cheap paintings she'd picked up over the years. She continued to talk to herself as she showered then got dressed in plain tan pants with a green top. She left her hair in a long ponytail down her back. She shoved a peanut-butter sandwich into her mouth and quickly brewed a single cup of coffee she had to balance in a regular cup due to her forgetfulness. Had it not been raining, she might have gone on a hunt to find her old to-go cup. But the gray day and steady drizzle put the kibosh on that plan. With Mr. Whitfield's umbrella at the ready, she stepped outside.

Thanks to a mechanism that operated like a well-oiled machine, Maggie was able to slide the umbrella open with ease. She smiled, lifted it over her head, and almost skipped to her car. She said a silent thank-you to Mr. Whitfield.

But when she arrived at the bookshop, something didn't look right. First of all, the front door was wide open.

Immediately, Maggie assumed that Joshua, in his infinite wisdom, had left the door open in order to haul something in. As she feared, the carpet at the entrance was soaked.

"Great," she muttered. There was a plastic runner behind the counter specifically for the rainy days, which did have a tendency to pile one on top of another at times. "But far be it from the new boss to ask any questions. Nope, just leave the door open and let everything get wet." She shook her head as she folded the umbrella with ease and stepped inside.

With her temper rising, she stomped over to the counter, where she dropped her purse and umbrella before grabbing the runner. It was rolled up tightly and wedged into the corner behind a ream of paper and a couple of boxes of paper receipt rolls and pens.

With her mind racing with the myriad of things she was going to scold Joshua about, she almost walked past the body on the floor.

As if her shirt had snagged on a nail, she stopped and eased back to take another look. It had to be just a trick of the light. There wasn't a body there. There were boots, attached to a pair of legs that led up to a torso. Maggie froze as her eyes met the dead stare of Bo Logan.

Maggie screamed.

It only took a few minutes for the police, paramedics, and fire department to arrive.

"You've had a rough week, Maggie," Officer Gary Brookes said as he walked into the shop and found her sitting on her usual stool out of the way behind the counter. "Are you all right? I meant to make it to Mr. Whitfield's service but had to work. No rest for the weary. My condolences. He was a good man."

Maggie knew Officer Brookes well. They'd gone to high school together.

"Thanks, Gary," she replied and wrinkled her face with the discomfort of having to talk to someone. Even though she knew Gary and he'd always been nice to her, she had very little to say to him. He was barrel-chested even without his bulletproof vest and had a couple tattoos snaking up his arms. He rode a Harley in his spare time. What would she ever have in common with him? Except this dead person they both knew.

"You want to tell me what happened here?" he asked without being pushy.

Maggie told Gary exactly what had happened. In fact, she repeated it a couple times as if she were trying to convince herself that it had, in fact, happened, that Bo was lying there on the floor dead.

"Looks like he might have gotten a jolt of juice," one of the paramedics said.

"Electrocution? That doesn't sound right," Maggie chirped. "He was a licensed electrician. Told me so himself. Well, not me directly, but I was there when he stopped Joshua from working on a light fixture. In fact, it was that one he's underneath." She pointed up to the ceiling, where some naked wires were sticking out. "He shut off the breaker."

"What's going on?" Joshua walked into the shop just as the paramedics were covering Bo and loading him onto a gurney.

"You left the door open. The whole entrance is wet," Maggie muttered.

"So you called the cops?" Joshua looked around at everyone.

"You're Joshua Whitfield? Alex's son?" Gary asked.

"I am, Officer. What happened?" Joshua asked.

Before anyone said anything, the paramedics wheeled Bo's body out of the bookshop.

As Gary talked to Joshua, Maggie got down off the stool and walked carefully around the counter. No one was paying much attention to her as she slowly wandered down the first aisle of books. On the floor was a pile of the older books Mr. Whitfield had collected, tossed there as if someone had been looking for something.

Slowly, Maggie turned around to see if she could catch Gary's attention, but he was busy taking notes from Joshua. She knelt and looked over the titles. Having read more than her fair share of mysteries, Maggie didn't touch anything. These books had come from one of the higher shelves but not the highest, where she was hiding all the antiquities that had more sentimental than monetary value. But only someone looking for them intentionally could have pulled these down. It wasn't like the books Joshua had kicked over the other night. She hated to leave them there on the floor.

"Gary?" She wrinkled her nose as he turned his head in her direction. She pointed to the floor. "Did you see this?"

He walked over and looked at the pile of books. "What am I looking at?"

"A pile of books. They were pulled down from the shelf," Maggie replied casually.

"So?" Gary waited for the punchline.

"Someone was in here looking for something." She shrugged.

"You said the door was wide open when you got here. Maybe a customer wandered in and…" Gary replied.

"First, it's not even seven in the morning, and we don't open until nine," Maggie said. "Second, you know darn well that even if we did open at six in the morning, no one in this town would be waiting for the door to open so they could quickly abscond with a fourth-edition copy of *Peyton Place*. I mean, be serious." Maggie almost laughed.

Just then, Poe appeared from the stairwell to investigate the commotion himself. He hopped up onto the bookcase, knocking more than one book on the floor before disappearing between the shelves so he could continue sneaking around. Maggie pouted before looking at Gary. She knew exactly what he was thinking.

"You always were weird, Maggie," Gary said before he turned and went back to Joshua, who had been listening with a frown.

Maggie went ahead and picked up the books. With her arms full, she grabbed the ladder and carefully stepped up to replace them on the shelf where they belonged.

"Are you the only one with a key, Mr. Whitfield?" Gary asked.

"No. Maggie has one. But I gave my key to Bo, because he said that he'd be able to get the majority of the wiring work done before the rest of his crew came in. He'd been coming in early for the past couple of days," Joshua said.

"I think we can cross Maggie off our list of suspects," Gary said.

"Hold on. Did you say suspects?" Joshua's eyes nearly popped out of his head. "Do you think someone intentionally hurt Bo?"

"I don't know, Joshua. It's just hard to ignore that some strange things have happened since you got to town," Gary replied.

"Strange things? Like what?" Joshua snapped.

"Like finding a dead guy in your bookstore," Gary replied.

"That's the café. This is the bookstore," Maggie corrected. When no one invited her to continue in the conversation, she shrugged and muttered to herself.

"Not to mention the rain picked up as soon as you got here," Gary replied.

"Are you serious? You're going to blame me for the rain?" Joshua shook his head. "I knew my father lived in a simple little town, but I didn't think you all were superstitious. Tell me, do you lock all the teenage girls inside when there's a full moon? Do you have some old broad in town who will read the bottom of your coffee cup for ten bucks?"

"That'll do, Joshua," Gary replied.

"Forgive me if I'm not in the mood to cooperate any further. The only decent electrician in town is dead, and you think I killed him? What could possibly be the reason?" Joshua asked.

"You tell me," Gary replied.

"No. I'm not telling you anything. I've told you everything I know. Margaret's the one who found him. Ask her," Joshua said before shouldering past Gary and heading upstairs to the apartment.

Without flinching, Gary walked up to Maggie and tucked his notebook back into his pocket.

"You don't really think Joshua had anything to do with this?" Maggie huffed.

"I don't know. I've never worked a murder case before. Where is the circuit board?" he asked.

Maggie led him around back to the small storeroom, which was accessible from both the new café side and the bookshop. Maggie wished she hadn't seen what she had seen. But all the switches to the café were in the off position so the guys could work—all but one. The one Bo had been working on was the only one in the on position.

"Looks odd, don't you think?" Gary said.

"Yeah, but it doesn't prove Joshua did anything," Maggie replied. "Even if they did have an argument yesterday."

"What about?" Gary asked.

Maggie gave him a quick version of what had happened. Even as she related the incident, she didn't think it was enough to push Joshua to murder. She didn't think anyone related to Alexander Whitfield, whether he read or not, could be capable of such a thing. Plus, if anything happened to Joshua, she would be out of a job.

There were plenty of weirdos in Fair Haven. Any number of them could have finally snapped and set Bo up. The possibilities were as vast and diverse as the books in the shop. Maggie was going to have to push aside her own suspicions. Joshua was the only one who knew Bo had been coming in early. But if there was anything she'd learned from the books she'd read, it was that the most obvious answer wasn't always the correct one.

## Chapter 8

The rain had not stopped for more than twenty-four hours. In fact, some of the locals who stepped into the bookshop to get out of the rain and have a quick peek at the gruesome death scene mentioned that the two bridges that led out of town had already flooded. Anyone who was visiting had no choice but to extend their stay until things got a little drier.

The news of Bo's death had spread as fast as the water running down the ditches into the drainage pipes. Only a couple of the men who had been on Bo's crew showed up to finish the job. They managed to get the light fixtures attached with no problems. Maggie had to admit they had transformed the empty furniture store into a fine café. Even she could see it would be quaint and lovely with some paint and decorations.

She stood in the doorway that joined the two places, her arms full of the new inventory Joshua had insisted she buy.

"Are you putting those on display in the window?" Joshua asked as he passed, his tool belt clanking against his hip and his boots clunking on the floor.

"Yes."

"Just stack them there. I want as many as you can cram in

the window so people know we are selling them," he replied. He looked down at the cans of wood varnish that were on the floor.

"I thought you wanted a nice display," Maggie replied.

"I do. But I need to get things moving. We're having a reveal party in just a few days, and this place has to be ready. So, chop-chop," Joshua said.

"Did you just say '*chop-chop*' to me?" she asked. How could this rogue have been sired by such a kind and gentle heart? For heaven's sake, what was his mother like? She had to be the cranky one of the bunch. Maggie was sure of it.

"I did," he replied.

Maggie pinched her lips together, clutched the books tight, and was about to go put the finishing touches on her display in the window when she heard something by the back door.

Every storefront had a back exit that led to the alley. Maggie was about to push the heavy door open when she realized it was already open. She saw a slim shaft of light from outside and felt a cool, wet draft immediately. Carefully, she pushed the door open and looked into the alley. There wasn't much trash, and it wasn't uncommon for someone to cut through the gangway from Pearson Street. But just as she was about to pull the door shut, she heard footsteps.

Maggie peeked around the door, screwing up her face as the drops of rain quickly found her. That was when she saw the umbrella.

"Hey, who is that?" she called to the person standing in the alley with her back to her.

The person turned around, and it was poor Ruby Sinclair. Maggie let out a sigh.

"There's fourteen. Fourteen of these and then eight more turns. I'll flip the switches and give another five turns. I have to tap-tap-tap…"

Poor Ruby Sinclair was weird. She had more money than the Toonsleys but lived in a messy Cape Cod–style home by herself. From what people said, she suffered from a form of obsessive-compulsive disorder that often had her wandering into people's open garages or opening and closing car doors. She would tap on windows and hop on sewer covers.

"Hi, Ruby," Maggie said as the woman continued to mutter.

Ruby waved but continued to mutter more to herself than for anyone to understand.

"It's nasty outside. Do you want to come in for a second and dry off?" Maggie asked.

"The switches. I'll flip the switches and give another five turns. Then I'll tap-tap-tap," Ruby muttered. She was wearing an expensive-looking dress that had gotten frayed around the edges. Her hair was graying at the roots, and her eyes were surrounded by wrinkles from being in the sun so much of the time.

"Yeah, come on in out of the rain for a few minutes." Maggie held the door open.

As if she'd been inside the bookstore a million times, Ruby folded her umbrella and sauntered in. But then Ruby did something that made Maggie's breath catch in her throat. She walked over to the fuse box. It had been closed and a little brass lock put on it to keep it safe from curious hands.

"The switches. I'll flip the switches," Ruby said. "That'll get things going nicely."

"No. You can't," Maggie replied and wondered if Ruby had slipped into the store and flipped the switch while Bo was working. He never would have seen her. And if the back door were open like it was now, she could have wandered in.

In a huff, as if all she'd ever wanted was to flip some fuses back and forth, Ruby looked down her nose at Maggie. She squared her shoulders and folded her hands politely in front of her before taking a deep breath.

"My father will hear about this," she scoffed, putting her right hand to her throat as if to clutch a string of pearls. With all the flair of a silent movie actress, she swept her other arm in front of her and walked out of the bookshop and back into the rain. With just as much grace, she pressed the button on the plastic umbrella handle, and it blossomed perfectly. Then Maggie watched as she hopped on the manhole cover three times before leaving the alley.

"Your father's been dead for two decades, but okay," Maggie muttered before shutting the door. Part of her wanted to let poor Ruby just go about her business. She was harmless, and in all her years of roaming Fair Haven, she'd never hurt or scared anyone. Even at her most eccentric, she managed to decorate her house for Christmas and keep the yard tidy all summer. She was just weird.

*But if she accidentally did this, it means she might hurt herself or someone else.* Maggie's thoughts flew. *Plus, that would mean that Joshua is in the clear, and maybe the crew will come back, and he'll be happy. Not that you care if he's happy. Why would you care about that? You just need this job.*

Right. It was her duty to tell Officer Gary Brookes about Ruby. She grabbed the big umbrella Mr. Whitfield had given her and left the shop without anyone noticing.

As she walked down the street, she inhaled the cool, damp air. The rain was steady, but it wasn't a storm as it had been the previous night. Cars slowly rolled past on the slick pavement with their windshield wipers lazily slapping back and forth. The lights of the other storefronts were a warm and inviting contrast to the gloominess of the day. Maggie felt the drops of rain that managed to sneak under the edge of her umbrella speckle her neck with tiny chilly kisses.

She wondered if Ruby Sinclair had any idea what she'd done.

"You don't know if she did it, Mags. You only have a suspicion because she was acting suspiciously. But she always acts suspiciously. Every day. That doesn't mean she did anything," Maggie mumbled as she walked, oblivious to the looks she was getting from the few other pedestrians, who would have thought her just as goofy if not kin to Ruby Sinclair.

"Maggie! Margaret Bell!"

The shouting behind her made Maggie whirl around with a frown. Who would be shouting her name? Loudly! Out in public? She narrowed her eyes at the barrel-shaped man waving and waddling quickly in her direction. For a second, she squinted as the man in the wide-brimmed Stetson hat and tweed blazer approached. But it took just a few more steps for her to recognize Mr. Toby Hodgkin.

Tobias S. Hodgkin was one of the few people Maggie would come out of her shell for. He'd been coming to the bookstore ever since she had started working there and told grand stories, some of which were as exciting as the short-story collections on the shelves. He had met all kinds of people and seen so many sights that she often wondered where he actually called home. England seemed to be his favorite place, but it was one of many. Unlike Mr. Whitfield, who was much more reserved and spoke quietly, Toby was a lion tamer in comparison. If Allan Quatermain ever needed some tips, Maggie would suggest he speak with Toby. If he weren't a fictional character.

"Hi, Toby!" Maggie finally smiled as she recognized the older man.

"I'm so sorry. I meant to get here in time for Alexander's wake. The weather," he said and shrugged sadly.

"You didn't miss anything, Toby. It wasn't like I expected him to wake up and scold us all for being ninnies," Maggie said.

"That would be exactly what he would say. Oh, who will I play chess with on my visits to town? Tell me, what's happening with the shop?" Toby asked as he offered Maggie his elbow like an old-fashioned gentleman.

"His son has come to take over," Maggie replied.

"You don't sound all that impressed. Is he not what you expected?" Toby asked.

Maggie rolled her eyes. "Toby, you knew Mr. Whitfield. He was a very well-educated man. Self-taught. Humble and kind with a sense of humor. Joshua doesn't even read. He wears blue jeans and has this tendency to run his hand through his hair every couple of minutes so he looks like James Dean. And he talks with the construction crew like they've been friends for years. He made me order some of the most horrible titles to display in the window to get more customers. He hasn't even read them. He just thinks since they are popular, they must be good. Who thinks like that? Talk about judging a book by its cover," Maggie said. She continued lamenting her dilemma in working for Joshua Whitfield for several more minutes.

"You know, Miss Mags, I once had a professor at university who asked the class if we thought any of the works of art at the Louvre didn't belong." He reached into his pocket and withdrew a pack of gum. He continued speaking as he offered a stick to Maggie. "Well, of course, yours truly immediately raised his hand and decried the fact that Winslow Homer's *Summer Squall* would be better suited for a fish-and-chips pub in Piccadilly Square," Toby said. "I prattled on and on, and when I was finished, I was certain that my professor would nod his head in agreement. Instead, he said, 'Tobias, the true purpose of art is to promote thought, discussion, stir emotion. You just proved why Homer's *Summer Squall* should most definitely be at the Louvre.'" Toby looked down at Maggie.

"Your point?" Maggie asked, wrinkling her nose as if she smelled something peculiar.

"My point, Mags, is that you sure do have a lot to say about a fellow who you claim has not the slightest appealing quality." Toby winked.

"Oh, aren't you horrible." Maggie tugged his arm as Toby laughed.

"That is something Alex always worried about. You clung to his side so faithfully that he felt a little guilty." Toby patted her hand. "Wouldn't he just be delighted gazing down from his heavenly perch to see his favorite gal Friday take an interest in his son?" Toby laughed again.

"I think you've been drinking already this morning," Maggie teased back, her cheeks flushing red.

"Where are you off to, my dear?"

"The police station," she said.

"Oh, I do hope my teasing hasn't made you decide to turn me in to the authorities," Toby gasped.

"I should. But no. I just need to talk to one of the officers. After Mr. Whitfield passed, we had an accident at the shop." She was happy to tell Toby about Bo, not because she was happy about what had happened but because she would have talked about anything to get off the topic of Joshua.

"My, what a spell of bad luck," Toby replied, clicking his tongue and shaking his head.

"You said a mouthful, Toby," Maggie said as they continued their walk together under Maggie's umbrella.

"I'm afraid I'll have to part with you here, my dear. I'm staying at the one and only bed-and-breakfast in town. Do you think the rain will ever subside? I'm stuck here until it does due to the bridges being underwater and Noah not having yet completed the ark," Toby said.

"I hate to tell you, but it's not going to stop for several days. But that's okay. Please come by the shop. I may not be as worthy an opponent as Mr. Whitfield, but I know where the chessboard is," Maggie replied.

"That sounds delightful. I'll be by in short order," Toby said before tipping his hat and heading off down Peterson Street in the direction of the bed-and-breakfast.

Maggie waved and was glad to have chatted with Toby. He had been one of Mr. Whitfield's oldest and dearest friends. They would spend hours talking together, debating, and laughing whenever Toby came to town. He travelled extensively, a man of adventure and knowledge. Well, maybe not so much adventure these days, as he was in his late sixties. But that didn't seem to stop him from seeing the world. Last time he'd arrived in Fair Haven, he had been returning from Dubai. Prior to that, he'd been in Finland. What he did for a living Maggie wasn't exactly sure. But whatever it was, it allowed him many luxuries.

# Chapter 9

"**M**aggie Bell, the last time I checked, you didn't complete training at the police academy," Officer Gary Brookes said as they sat together at his desk. He was behind it with serious stacks of files to his right and his left. Maggie was in front of it with her hands folded in her lap.

"I never said I did. But I ran into Ruby today, and she was acting peculiar." Maggie wrinkled her nose.

"You know, you are so adorable when you do that," Gary teased.

"Do what?"

"Wrinkle your nose. You do it whenever something aggravates you. Like right now." Gary chuckled. When he saw Maggie wasn't laughing too or even the slightest bit amused, he cleared his throat and leaned forward toward her.

"I'm being serious, Gary," Maggie said.

"I know you are. And I do appreciate your help. But if I were to run Ruby Sinclair in every time she acted unusually weird, I'd have the poor woman in here at least four times a month. She's harmless," Gary replied.

"But you did see the fuse box. All the switches for that part of the building were off but the one Bo was working on. She was going on and on about flipping switches. With her condition being so severe, she might not have been able to help herself." Maggie spoke quietly and barely let her eyes stray from the top of Gary's desk to his face. She didn't want to know if anyone was looking at her or listening to what she was saying.

"Yes. I saw the fuse box. Let me ask you this. A person like Ruby, do you think she'd be content to just flip one switch in the middle of all those fuses? I think that would drive her crazier than not flipping any." Gary shrugged. "But hey, for your first murder, it was as good a try as any."

Maggie smirked. "It's your first murder too."

"Yeah, don't remind me. So, how are you doing? You okay?" Gary asked.

"I'm fine. Except that Joshua Whitfield made me order thirty-five copies of *Autumn at Dawn* to display in the window," Maggie said, waiting for Gary to gasp in horror. When he frowned and shook his head, she huffed, "Never mind."

"Hey, if you think of anything else, just stop by. Or even if you don't. I rarely get people to come in who don't have some kind of complaint," Gary urged.

Maggie wrinkled her nose then remembered what he'd said and instantly stopped. When she looked at Gary, she couldn't help but smile. He chuckled again and waved as she left.

When she got back to the bookstore, her shoes were soaked. The weather had picked up in the last few blocks of her journey, and when she stepped inside the bookshop, Joshua was waiting for her as if she'd stayed out with a boy past her curfew.

"Where were you?" he snapped.

"What?" she replied back. She hadn't even had a chance to fold her umbrella and stow it in the corner to drip dry.

"I'm asking where you were. This place is scheduled to open in less than a week, and I need you here doing your job.

If you are going to take an early lunch, then you need to let me know," Joshua said as he shifted from one foot to the other.

"Did we have any customers?" she asked with surprise.

"No."

"Did someone come looking for Mr. Whitfield?"

"No. I think I could handle someone coming to look for my father," Joshua replied.

"So no one came in. There were no customers. But you needed me here to handle the…?" Maggie shrugged before walking around the counter to take her usual seat on the tall stool.

Joshua put his hands in his back pockets. "I'm sorry. I'm… not being fair. Things just aren't going the way they are supposed to. But they never do. College. My marriage. Now this. What was I expecting?"

Maggie suddenly felt bad not just for Joshua but for her behavior too. "No. You're right. I should have told you I was running an errand. Your father gave me a lot of freedom. Old habits are hard to break."

"Isn't that the truth?" Joshua smiled. "Believe it or not, he always talked about you in his letters. Ever since my mom died, I was really afraid for him being alone. But I don't think he ever was. If it wasn't you he was talking about, it was one of the old coots he sold his books to."

"Your father was very well liked. Everyone in town knew him," Maggie said before feeling a sting in her eyes. The last thing she wanted to do was cry in front of Joshua. She quickly busied herself by getting down off the stool and picking up one of the shipments of new books that had arrived.

"Let me get that." Joshua rushed to her side and took the box as if it was loaded with feathers.

"Thanks," Maggie said, still looking down as if she were checking for something else.

"How's the window coming?" Joshua asked.

"It'll be ready for your party. Don't worry," Maggie replied.

"I'm not worried. Can I set the box on the window ledge?" he asked politely.

"That would be great," Maggie said.

She walked over to the display window, which was partially covered with the sheets Joshua had stapled up for her. She stepped up into the display area and held the curtain back. Joshua joined her and placed the box on the window ledge. It held a small table and a chair and not much else.

"I know it doesn't look like much yet," Maggie said quietly.

"This is a nice little fort you've got here," Joshua tried to joke. He stood straight and towered over her by at least six inches. Maggie could smell his cologne and liked the clank his tool belt made when he shifted his feet.

"I might come back after hours and just sit in here and read with a flashlight," she said, thinking her own idea of fun sounded extra nerdy at the moment. What did Joshua do for fun? He probably went rock climbing or extreme bicycling or something she'd never be able to do.

"I'll bring the sleeping bags," Joshua chuckled, his smile wide and innocent.

Maggie couldn't say the idea of camping out on the floor of the bookstore with Joshua Whitfield didn't sound like a small slice of heaven. She blinked as she looked up at him, and her cheeks turned bright red. After swallowing hard, she looked down at the floor.

"I better get back to work," she said and quickly stepped down from the display window to grab a box cutter from the drawer.

"Yeah, me too." Joshua cleared his throat and adjusted his tool belt. "These books will really make a difference."

Maggie couldn't stop herself from grunting.

"Something wrong?" Joshua asked.

"No. You said to get these books and put them in the display. That's what I'm doing," Maggie replied with a crooked smile.

"But you don't think it's a good idea?" Joshua pressed.

"You are the boss," Maggie replied and put her hands up. "I guess I just liked the books your dad suggested better."

"Tell me one," Joshua replied, making Maggie freeze.

"What?"

"Tell me one of the books my dad told you to read," Joshua said.

He was shocked to see Maggie dash to the back of the bookstore and return with an old book with yellowed pages and red cover with gold-leaf lettering.

"This is a first edition of Ian Fleming's *Casino Royale*. James Bond. Now, I'm not really a big James Bond fan, but the movies all started here. I have to say, if your dad hadn't forced me to read this, I probably would never have known who James Bond even was," Maggie chirped.

Joshua couldn't help but notice how Maggie came out of her protective and grumpy shell when he asked her such a simple question about books. She smiled as she talked and looked around the room. But suddenly, as if she was reading his thoughts, she stopped.

"I'm babbling," she said.

"No. I think I understand a little bit better what you were saying," Joshua replied.

"Well, here. Maybe you could try reading this." She handed him the book.

"Maybe I will," he said as he watched her step back up into her fort.

"There will be a test on it," Maggie replied from behind the sheet. She heard Joshua laugh before he walked to the other side of the wall to continue his work in the café. She shook her head. Could she have sounded any more pathetic? *There will be a test on it? Really?*

## Chapter 10

The next day, Maggie decided she was going to avoid Joshua as much as possible. He'd distracted her the previous day, and she felt she had made a fool of herself trying to be cute by showing him the old copy of *Casino Royale*. He had to think she was a big nerd, and even if he didn't, she was positive there was no reason for her to try to impress him. He was nothing like his father, and that was too bad. But he was her boss, and if she was going to keep her job, she'd just do as she was told and keep the small talk to a minimum.

"It doesn't look like Joshua is going to tend to his father's desk," Maggie muttered to herself. "That's probably for the best. He'll just make a mess of things."

As Maggie started to go through the letters and invoices on the desk, she saw how very little money the store was actually making and how costly it was to keep open. Mr. Whitfield had never complained once about the money or even mentioned bills to her. He paid her faithfully every two weeks, with a small bonus each Christmas season. She wished she had known the true state of affairs. But it was too late now.

As she rummaged through the first stack, she came across

a letter from Toby. But what she read shocked her to her core. The nice old man she'd just joked and walked with, who had come to Fair Haven for Mr. Whitfield's funeral, called him a cheat and a liar.

*ALEXANDER,*

*It is with a heavy heart I even write this letter. The fact our decades-long friendship means so little to you of all people is like a dagger in my back. I've not asked you for many favors, Alex, and any monies I may owe you will all be paid in full as they always have been. I am merely asking you to help a friend in their time of need. But I should have known that there are certain things that test the boundaries of friendship. You wouldn't even allow me to see the book on my last visit. Like my very gaze may take away some of its value. It was a sad day for me to discover my good friend to be a liar and a cheat. But mark my words, old man. Those things you cherish will not go to the grave with you. And no one will think anything of a friend requesting a few items to remember such a long alliance.*
*You are a stubborn old man and will pay the price as Miser did. It will be at your funeral and no sooner that I'll see you again.*
*—Tobias*

MAGGIE COULD HARDLY BELIEVE her eyes. And the letter was dated four months ago. It wasn't as if it was a tiff that had taken place years ago and been resolved. This had to have been fresh in Toby's mind when he was walking with her. He'd said nothing. He'd shown no remorse. In fact, he'd played along like a heartbroken friend who would have just come by to ask for one or two of Mr. Whitfield's books, which Maggie would have happily given him.

What was this about? If Mr. Whitfield had had a reason

not to give away one of his books, she wanted to know what it was. And she was not afraid to confront Toby head on. But she couldn't just up and leave like she'd done yesterday, and she didn't want to go up to Joshua and ask. Her nerves jittered at the very thought of it. She'd just have to wait until quitting time.

The hours crawled by. Maggie slit open the boxes to reveal the corny image of a young woman staring dopily ahead with the arm of a mysterious man around her and the title *Autumn at Dawn* in a tacky cursive-style font. It had the gold stamp of embossed letters stating it was a *New York Times* No. 1 Bestseller.

Maggie pulled them out of the box as if they might be contaminated with some unknown germ. Without realizing it, she frowned through the whole process. But when she stood back from her display and looked at it, she was happy with how her vision was coming to life. And as much as she hated to admit it, she was having fun. She had always had fun when Mr. Whitfield was around. If they weren't chatting pleasantly, she was allowed to read. What wasn't to like about that? But a certain satisfaction came with a hard day of work.

When she looked at the brass clock behind the counter, it was five o'clock. Without a moment's hesitation, she stopped what she was doing, came out of her cocoon, quickly grabbed her purse and umbrella, and left, locking the bookshop door behind her. She couldn't help but recall Mr. Sherlock Holmes in *The Adventure of the Abbey Grange*. *"Come, Watson, come! The game is afoot! Not a word! Into your clothes and come!"*

## Chapter 11

With the horrible letter in her pocket, Maggie marched off, as angry as the rain that continued to fall steadily. The drops on the vinyl of the umbrella made a constant pat-pat-pat sound that mingled with the "sheesh" of the cars rolling past on the street.

Fair Haven's most distinguished bed-and-breakfast was a six-room Victorian house with a spire and a wraparound porch. Mrs. Antonia Scucci and her husband, Sal, had started the business out of their home after the last of their six children had left.

Maggie walked into the foyer, folded her umbrella, and shook it out a little before leaning it against the wall with a couple others that were drying. She pulled open the etched-glass door and stepped into the parlor, where Mrs. Scucci was standing behind her counter. In all the years Maggie had known the Scuccis, she'd never seen Mrs. Scucci without at least a dozen gold chains around her neck. Her fingers were just as decorated, with rings on all her fingers. Her hair was dyed black, and her strong nose gave her an elegant Italian look.

"*Buonasera*, Maggie." Mrs. Scucci waved.

"Hi, Mrs. Scucci," Maggie replied. She quickly looked to the sitting area of the parlor and let out a quiet sigh of relief that there was no one else there. She and Mrs. Scucci were alone.

"I'm so sorry about Mr. Whitfield." Mrs. Scucci made the sign of the cross over herself. "He was a good man, God rest his soul."

"Thank you," Maggie replied with a soft smile.

"I see his son has come to town," Mrs. Scucci said. "I also heard he is *divorziato*."

Maggie pouted out her lips and shrugged.

"You want I should cook up an old Italian potion my grandmother gave me? It will lure him to you to love you forever." Mrs. Scucci nodded.

Maggie laughed. "No, Mrs. Scucci."

"Are you sure? It's how I got my Sal." Mrs. Scucci jerked her thumb over her shoulder toward the door that led to their kitchen. "A lifetime of headache. Why would you say no to that?"

Again, Maggie laughed as she leaned against the counter. "That's okay, Mrs. Scucci. I'm wondering if Mr. Hodgkin is in?"

"He's a little old for you." Mrs. Scucci frowned.

"Are you serious? He's Mr. Whitfield's friend." Maggie nearly choked on those words as she thought of the letter he had written.

"He's staying here, but he just left about ten minutes ago for dinner," Mrs. Scucci said as she waved toward the door.

Just then, a loud crash and a long string of Italian words came pouring from the kitchen.

"What are you doing?" Mrs. Scucci shouted as she turned and went into the kitchen.

"I forgot the plate was hot!" Sal replied and then added a few more words in Italian.

Maggie looked at the register in front of her. Quickly, she

spun it around and caught a glimpse of Toby's room number. He was staying in room four. After turning the book around, she quickly hurried up the stairs to where the rooms were.

The Scuccis' home was beautiful, with aged photos of family from "the old country" taking up every bit of space on the walls. The floors were nicked and scratched hardwood with area rugs and runners strategically placed down the hallway and in front of each guest's door. The boards of the stairs and hallway creaked under her weight, making her hope she wasn't sounding some alarm to Mrs. Scucci that someone was roaming the hallway uninvited.

So Maggie hurried to door number four and pressed her ear against it. She heard nothing stirring inside and hoped that in such a quiet town, Toby knew well he might ignore the notion of locking his room. She gripped the old-fashioned glass doorknob and gave it a twist.

Without hindrance, the door opened. Maggie quickly looked both ways down the hallway then stuck her head inside.

"Hello? Toby?" she whispered then held her breath. Nothing.

Without waiting another second, Maggie stepped inside the room and closed the door tightly behind her. The room was dark, with the curtains closed tightly, and it took a second for her eyes to adjust. Once they did, Maggie hurried to the elegant little desk next to the window and snapped on the small lamp sitting there. It gave off just enough light for her to see the room was indeed empty.

Toby's suitcases and toiletry bag were on the bed. It did look as if he'd just arrived, as he'd said. There was also a briefcase. Maggie carefully snapped the locks open. Inside, she found several legal documents with Toby's name on them. They made no sense to her as she skimmed them, looking for Mr. Whitfield's name. Her first thought was that Toby was going to take legal action against her late boss or his estate or

Joshua. Perhaps he was going to try to secure Mr. Whitfield's library as his own. But it didn't look that way, since the documents mentioned neither Alex nor Joshua.

Instead, they all mentioned Toby and threatened legal action if certain debts were not paid or repayment plans were not agreed upon. As she continued digging, she saw at least three credit card statements with more than thirty thousand dollars in debt shown on the total line. The charges had not been incurred in the exotic locations she would have expected; they were from the Golden Nugget Casino, the Bellagio Hotel, the Flamingo, all in Las Vegas. Maggie swallowed hard. Then she saw an old receipt that looked familiar. It was from the bookshop in Mr. Whitfield's handwriting.

"To be delivered upon receipt of payment in full" was what it said. It was for a first-edition copy of William Faulkner's *The Sound and the Fury*. The price was $10,200. That was one of the books Maggie had stashed behind the rows in order to make sure Joshua didn't throw it away accidentally, thinking it was a worthless old title. But even Maggie had to gasp at what it was worth. She'd had no idea. It had never even crossed her mind to look into the value of the books in Mr. Whitfield's library. She'd thought they were priceless because of their stories and the memories she had of discussing them with her friend.

From the looks of things, Toby had gambled away a fortune. It looked as if the book was something he could have used to pay off some of the debt. But Mr. Whitfield hadn't given it to him. He'd expected to be paid first. Of course he had. Who wouldn't?

Before she could put everything back, she heard noises in the hallway. Toby's deep voice was unmistakable.

"Thank you, Mrs. Scucci! I'll do just that!" Toby called down the stairs.

Maggie ran to the door. Her body trembled. What would she say? She could hide under the bed, but what if he stayed in the room the rest of the night? As her mind raced, she saw the old lock, just a flat brass switch that would open with the help of a skeleton key. Without thinking, Maggie snapped it into place. She braced herself against the wall and held her breath.

Within seconds, Toby grabbed hold of the doorknob and gave it a turn. Only it didn't turn. The lock was in place, buying Maggie a couple precious seconds—maybe a minute or two—to think. She ran to the window and looked outside. The continuous rain and slippery ledge quickly dashed any idea of escaping through the window.

"Mrs. Scucci?" Toby called. "Mrs. Scucci? It appears I've accidentally locked myself out of my room."

Maggie hurried on tiptoe back to the door and listened. She was sure she heard Toby's footsteps sounding off the symphony of creaks as he went back down the hall and downstairs. It was now or never.

She grabbed hold of the latch, turned it as quietly as she could, and opened the door. Her body rigid with nerves, she stepped out into the hallway, pulled the door shut behind her, sashayed to the nearest door across the hallway, turned the knob, and stepped inside. She shut the door behind her, dropped to her knees, and peeked beneath the door. She watched as Toby's shoes reappeared along with those of Mrs. Scucci, who was saying something so fast that Maggie couldn't tell if she was speaking English or Italian.

"*Voila!*" she exclaimed as the door opened.

"*Grazie*, Mrs. Scucci," Toby exclaimed.

"*Prego, prego*," Mrs. Scucci replied and walked away quickly.

Just as the door to Toby's room closed, Maggie got to her feet, quietly turned the doorknob, and opened the door. No one was in the hallway. With her nerves doing the jitterbug and her heart beating so fast she felt it in her fingertips, she stepped into the hallway, pulled the door shut, and tiptoed past Toby's room. Without worrying about the squeaky floor-boards, she went downstairs and carefully peeked around the banister to see if Mrs. Scucci was at her counter. The coast was clear.

With as much grace as a bulldog maneuvering under a kitchen table, Maggie made it to the door—after bumping into the side table, tripping on a flap of area rug, and fumbling with the doorknob into the foyer. For her final act, she grabbed her umbrella as she stepped outside into the rain and disappeared down the sidewalk.

## Chapter 12

The next day, Maggie arrived at work and saw more than a dozen boxes from various publishing houses piled in front of the counter. The new inventory had arrived. As Maggie unpacked the books, she wondered where they were supposed to go. She'd never be able to fit this many old titles on the shelves. Joshua or someone would notice if she crammed too many, and then what?

Then she had an idea that Joshua might consider. If he wanted people to be lured by the siren song of trendy, easy-to-read novels, then maybe having bookshelves on either side of the new door joining the café to the bookshop would be promising.

Without delay, Maggie went to find Joshua but stopped when she saw him standing in the back of the café with Officer Gary Brookes.

"I'm telling you that I wasn't anywhere near the shop when Bo died. Had I been here, I would have sent him home. He was doing me a favor. I had no reason to hurt him," Joshua said.

"I'm just telling you that we have a witness who said they saw you here at the store around the time Bo died and that you made tracks out of here quickly, like you were running from something," Gary said.

"Who? Who's telling you this?" Joshua snapped.

"I'm not at liberty to reveal that information at this time, but…" Gary started, but Joshua stopped him.

"If you aren't going to tell me the name of my accuser, then you better come back with something more solid. If I'm not being arrested, I'm going to politely ask you to leave." Joshua shook his head, put his hands on his hips and looked at the floor before nodding toward the door. "I've got a lot of work to do."

Gary clicked his tongue before turning and walking out the back exit to the alley.

Maggie hung back a few minutes so Joshua wouldn't think she was eavesdropping. Finally, she intentionally dropped a couple of books and muttered a few words just so he knew she was there.

"Margaret? Is that you?" he called.

"Yes!" she shouted back.

Just as she was about to go to him, Joshua appeared in the doorway and caused her to again drop the books that had been in her hands.

"I'm sorry. I didn't mean to scare you," Joshua said.

"It's okay. I'm a klutz." She wrinkled her face and shook her head. "Were you talking to someone? I thought I heard voices." Maggie fully expected Joshua to say no, that he hadn't been talking to anyone, and that maybe she'd heard his radio or he was just talking to himself. But he didn't.

"That was Officer Brookes. He says that someone saw me running away from here the night Bo was killed. The coroner pinpointed the time of death, and I was busy then. Nowhere near here. I'm telling you, I don't know how my father put up with the people in this town," Joshua said. "You read stories about people in small towns knowing everyone else's business. Well, Fair Haven fits that stereotype to a T."

74

"It can be kind of rough when you don't know people very well," Maggie replied.

She knew most of the people in town from a distance herself. No one ever said more to her than "How's Mr. Whitfield?" these days. And now that he had passed away, after enough grieving time had gone by, Maggie figured no one would speak to her at all. But her introverted nature saw no downside to that scenario.

"Tough? I'm being accused of murder. That's a little more intense than not being invited to the neighborhood block party."

"Do you have an alibi?" Maggie asked innocently.

"So what, do you think I killed Bo too?"

"No. I don't. I'm just saying that you don't have to be Agatha Christie to know a good alibi will do wonders if you are being accused of murder," Maggie snapped right back with an added eye roll for dramatic affect.

"You really have a serious attitude problem," Joshua said.

"I do? You're the one clomping around here, telling everyone what to do," Maggie replied, only to see Joshua smirk.

"That's because I'm the boss. This is my bookshop now and my café, and it's going to be my lounge in the evening too," Joshua said.

"Bar? What are you talking about now?" Maggie didn't know if she really wanted to hear what Joshua had to say. It seemed that every time he opened his mouth, it meant more bad news and uncomfortable moments coming her way.

"Once the café is up and running and we get the early birds and lunch crowd to come by, I thought it would be good to have a nice lounge for people to have a cocktail. Just wine and beer. No hard stuff. Maybe a couple festive coffees or a rum drink when the weather calls for it, but..."

"So, now we're going to be a bar?" Maggie pursed her lips.

"Yes, *we* are," Joshua replied. "No matter what Deputy Dog thinks or anyone else in this town. My dad's shop isn't going to get closed down because it isn't making any money, and I'm not going to invest my life savings in a ship destined to sink."

"Are the people who are drinking going to be able to come into the bookstore?" Maggie asked nervously. People who had alcohol had the tendency to talk more, and the last thing Maggie wanted was people around her talking more.

"If they want to," Joshua replied.

"Some of these books are valuable. If someone spills a glass of merlot on one of your father's copies of Charles Dickens, they've ruined it." Maggie shook her head.

"We'll have a 'You spill on it, you've bought it' policy. Will that make you happy?" Joshua replied. "Why do you have to fight me on everything? You are no different from anyone else in this town."

Maggie gasped. It was as if he had called her a string of things that would make a sailor blush.

"Your father thought I was fine the way I am. In fact, your father was the only one who thought that. He never made me feel self-conscious or nervous. Not like you and everyone else in this town. I've got work to do," Maggie snapped and bit back tears. "Put bookshelves of the new titles around the door. Maybe your trendy new crowd will find them more easily."

"That's a great idea," Joshua said as Maggie walked to the back of the store. When he considered what she had described, it really did seem to be a good idea. He felt terrible for talking to her the way he had.

The truth was that Maggie really was the only person in Fair Haven who had been honest with him from the second he'd shown up. She was a little prickly, yes, but there was something about her that he liked. Maybe it was just the fact that she was always there, reliable and steadfast. Or maybe it was how she wrinkled her nose when she was faced with a problem. He wondered if she wrinkled her nose when she laughed. Then it dawned on him that he hadn't seen her laugh. That made him feel all the more terrible. But what could he do now? He had deadlines and painting and a few last-minute details to tend to before the big unveiling. He'd have to deal with Maggie later. Right now, he had to make some phone calls and hope that Roger Hawes hadn't somehow gotten to Tammy and convinced her to sell her pastries to his construction workers, leaving Joshua with no coffee, no food, and no help.

## Chapter 13

W hen Maggie finally got home, she felt as if she'd been at the bookshop for twenty-four hours straight. When Mr. Whitfield had been alive, her days had never dragged on like this. She was so aggravated with Joshua that she didn't know what to do.

And as if hearing her thoughts loud and clear, as soon as Maggie had slipped into her pajamas for the night and was ready to cook some soup, her landlady was on the porch, her giant golf umbrella overhead making her look like a giant mushroom.

"Mrs. Peacock, are you all right?" Maggie asked.

"Yes, dear. I'm fine. I hear that Mr. Whitfield the younger is really making some drastic changes at the bookshop. So I am assuming that you will continue to work there?" She sounded more like she was giving a command than asking a question.

"Yes, I'll be working there," Maggie replied and tried to force a smile.

"Good. You have no idea how hard it is to find good tenants, and I'd hate to have to put you out on the street. But you know I'll do it. I'm on a fixed income, and I rely on your steady contribution to live," Mrs. Peacock said. "Without it, I shudder to think what could happen."

Mrs. Vivian Peacock had been telling Maggie she'd put her out on the street for the past six years. At first, Maggie had fretted about whether poor Mrs. Peacock was eating saltine crackers and drinking nothing but water as she lived from one rent check to the next. That went on until Mrs. Peacock invited Maggie to her annual Fourth of July celebration and the tenant saw the inside of her home. It was a beautiful place with dozens of pretty antiques as well as a few convincing knockoffs. The woman was rich. But she was cheap.

"Yes, well, if my situation changes, you'll be the first to know," Maggie said, hoping that would be enough to chase her landlady from her front door. Or maybe the rain could pick up or lightning could start flashing.

"I heard that Joshua Whitfield is a very handsome man and recently divorced," Mrs. Peacock said as subtly as a passenger train at rush hour.

"I wouldn't know about that," Maggie replied, looking down and then behind her into her little cottage that she wanted so desperately to be alone in.

"You wouldn't? Why, I heard he's told Tammy McCarthy that he'd have no idea what to do if it weren't for you," Mrs. Peacock said. "It's too bad he's being investigated."

"Investigated for what?" Maggie asked.

"For the death of my handyman. Oh, I don't believe it, but the rumors around town are hard to ignore. Bo knew how to do just about everything, and to make such a mistake as to forget to turn off the electricity, well, the man would rather have sliced off his own hand. You have to admit it is a queer situation." Mrs. Peacock nodded as she stared at Maggie, hoping for a wisp of gossip.

"I don't know anything about it," Maggie replied.

"You've not heard anything? You haven't spoken to Officer

Brookes? You two went to high school together, didn't you?"
Mrs. Peacock kept digging.

"Yes, we did," Maggie replied. "I didn't really know him.
Still don't."

"Oh, I see. Well, I think if Joshua Whitfield can manage to
clear his name, he might be a very promising prospect for you.
You really should go out more. I can't be responsible for you
the rest of my life. A young girl like you should be thinking of
her future."

Maggie twisted her face and let out a deep sigh, indicating
she wasn't at all comfortable with the conversation and more
than likely didn't believe it. "Mrs. Peacock, my dinner is on
the stove," Maggie lied. "Is there anything else?"

"No. Just good to know that your job is secure," Mrs.
Peacock said. "Oh, this rain is never going to stop. My whole
yard is going to have to be relandscaped. Lord knows I don't
have the money for that." She continued telling her tale of
woe to the raindrops as she quickly shuffled back to the big
house.

After mentioning it, Maggie decided she was hungry and
made herself a mug of tomato soup and a grilled cheese sandwich. As she stood next to the stove, she wondered who could
be saying such things about Joshua without even knowing all
the facts. As the heat from the burners chased any chills from
the gloomy weather from her body, Maggie thought of Toby's
cruel letter to Mr. Whitfield and the debt he was in. She
wondered if a confrontation was necessary after all. The
books had been knocked to the floor. Someone looking for a
specific title would have done that. Maybe Bo had seen him or
questioned why he was there after hours. Maggie didn't know.
But she was going to find out.

## Chapter 14

The next day, Maggie made the mistake of buying a sticky bun from Tammy's Bakery. They were one of her favorite guilty pleasures. But because of how sticky they were, no matter how hard she tried, she couldn't prevent the gooey frosting from getting on her face, so she ate them privately in the alley.

It would have been a simple task on a regular day, but maneuvering her umbrella with one hand and a sticky bun with the other was more than a little tricky. Just as she was about to turn the corner off the main street, already sinking her teeth into the gluey pastry and anticipating the protection from the awning over the back door, Maggie froze.

"We talked, Joshua," Samantha Toonsley purred. She was standing dangerously close to Joshua even though the awning offered enough room for at least three people. "You said that you had it and that you'd consider my offer. I'd like to know what's changed."

"Samantha, a lot has changed," Joshua replied. He was standing there in his tool belt, looking as good as he always did. Maggie hated that he was so darn handsome and how his hair fell over his forehead like James Dean's. Oh, who did he think he was?

"There are certain things that I can do to make this a better deal for you. Just name it," Samantha said and took a step closer to him.

Could she have been more obvious? Maggie knew what was on her mind and was shocked. Well, she really wasn't that shocked. There wasn't a man in all of Fair Haven who didn't notice Samantha Toonsley in any room she walked into. From what Maggie had heard, she worked out with a personal trainer at least three times a week. She had an open account at Spotlight Boutique, and she'd been heard bragging about having several of the exact same dresses as worn by some celebrities Maggie had never heard of. But that was not a surprise, since Maggie would always rather read the book than see the movie. However, this was the first time that Samantha had ever come to the bookstore in all the years Maggie had worked here.

"I'll bet you say that to all the guys," Joshua flirted back.

Maggie cringed. How could a guy fall for that? Sure, she was beautiful and built and had money but...what was Maggie even thinking? Of course a guy would fall for that.

"I might say it to them. But with you, I mean it." Samantha straightened Joshua's collar and let her hands linger there for a few seconds longer than they should have.

"What would Mr. Toonsley say?" Joshua asked.

Were they still playing a flirty game, or was there something more going on here? Maggie didn't know, and the gooey coating of her pastry was starting to solidify in the cooler air and make her fingers stick together. And she could already feel the same stickiness on her cheek, where she was sure her latest bite had smeared the stuff on her face.

"Mr. Toonsley doesn't even have to know about it. There are a number of things Mr. Toonsley doesn't know about, and look at how happy he is. You won't get any kind of argument

or complaining from him. I can promise you that," Samantha
said.

"It's very tempting, Samantha, but the answer is no,"
Joshua said without stepping back. He hooked his thumbs in
his tool belt and just stood there.

Samantha put her hands on her hips and gave the discussion one last try. "Do you even know who you are saying no
to?" she asked. "I'll tell you what. You can think about it.
Don't give me an answer right away. And I promise, if you are
willing to work with me, I'll make it worth your while. And I
promise to be discreet. The last thing I need is a couple of
competitors in town trying to horn in on my domain."

"I'm not your domain, Samantha. And no matter what,
the answer will be no," Joshua replied. The look on his face
was serious. The smirk was gone.

"You'll be sorry. I'll tell you that right now. Look, I'm
giving you one last chance and..." Samantha was not taking
rejection very well. Maggie thought it was probably the first
time in ages that someone had told her no.

But Maggie could no longer lurk around the corner with
her sticky treat melting into her hand. She took another bite
as she backed away from the alley, only to have a mob of
pedestrians on their way to work come hurrying past. Maggie
looked down to avoid eye contact. In one hand, she had a
useless napkin that was covered in sticky icing and stuck to the
umbrella handle. In the other was the rest of the sticky culprit.
A gust of wind blew a few strands of her hair from her ponytail across her face, and they stuck in place across her mouth
and cheek. It was gross, and she knew she looked a mess.

Like someone having some kind of tantrum as she walked
down the street, Maggie huffed and pouted, wrinkling her
nose as she made her way to the front of the bookshop and
hoping that Joshua hadn't forgotten to unlock the door.
Another gust of wind caught the umbrella, pulling her back
another step and a half and causing her to nearly poke the eye

out of some guy trying to get to work. When she finally gave the door an awkward push, her purse fell to her elbow, yanking down the umbrella and causing it to poke her on the top of her head and pull one strand of hair out at the root.

"Yeow!" Maggie yelped as she stepped inside.

Inside, looking rather bored, was a young man about twenty years old. He smirked at Maggie and made no attempt to help her with her umbrella or the door or anything else.

"Who are you? The store isn't open yet," Maggie huffed as she dropped the umbrella behind the counter. For a brief second, Maggie thought it was Joshua, as this stranger was as tall as him. He was maybe slightly thinner, but he had the same wide shoulders.

"Yeah, like I'd buy anything from this place," he grumbled, still smirking.

Maggie narrowed her eyes as she stared at him. It became obvious that he was related to Samantha Toonsley. They had the same blue eyes, high cheekbones, and smooth, slightly tanned skin. He wore an expensive-looking black jacket that hadn't a pet hair or stray fuzzy on any of it. His hair was blond and swept back from his face, professionally cut and styled to look slightly sloppy.

Before Maggie had a chance to tell the little twerp where he could get off, Samantha came crashing through the back of the store. She was so angry that with each step, Maggie could feel the ground shake and was sure the books she'd hidden between the shelves were going to come crashing down.

"What's the matter? Did you get it? Mom, did you get it?" the young man asked.

"No, Heath. I didn't get it. But I will," Samantha snapped as she pushed past Maggie only after giving her a judgmental look.

Maggie wrinkled her nose and felt the stickiness tug at the skin on her face.

Heath followed his mother. Maggie wasn't sure which one

of them had dived into a pool of designer fragrances, but the pungent scent was so strong it made her eyes water and a sneeze threaten to race down her nose at any second. It smelled like citrus fruit tainted with some cleaning product.

"What do you mean you didn't get it?" the young man shouted on the street. "You said you were going to. You told the Boddiggers you would have it."

"Well, I guess I'll have to tell the Boddiggers it's taking longer than I thought," Samantha replied.

"This is humiliating. I can't believe that you couldn't get it. I mean, what good is your collection without it? It's incomplete. Worthless," the younger Toonsley griped as they started to walk away.

"Ugh," she grumbled as the two Toonsleys left the front of the shop, leaving the strong scent in their wake.

Maggie hurried to the utility room in the corner of the bookshop, flipped the light on with her elbow, and dropped the remaining bite of her breakfast into the trashcan. She didn't have an appetite anymore. When she looked at her face, she just sighed. Somewhere along her journey from the alley to the front door, she had managed to get a smudge of dirt in addition to the gooey frosting down the side of her cheek.

"You look like you were hit by a train," she huffed. She turned on the faucet, set her glasses on the sink, and pumped some soap into her hand.

"Who's back there?" Joshua shouted.

"Just me!" Maggie replied. She worked up a lather and cleaned her hands before leaning over the sink to tackle her face. Just as she finished scrubbing, when she looked up into the mirror, Joshua was standing behind her.

"That's a good look for you, Margaret," he teased.

"Oh!" she huffed. "It's not like this utility closet offers any kind of privacy."

"Yikes, looks like this room will have to be updated next," Joshua said. He stepped closer to Maggie, who was quickly rinsing her face. "We should make this into a powder room. The piping is already here. What's your favorite color?"

"What?" Maggie looked at him strangely as she grabbed what was nothing more than a paper napkin from the edge of the sink and dried her face before slipping her glasses back on.

"Your favorite color. What is it?"

"Why?" Maggie leaned back as if a trapdoor might snap open beneath her feet if she wasn't careful.

"Because I want to know. It's not a trick question." Joshua's annoyance could hardly be disguised as he shook his head.

"Red," Maggie finally said.

"Really?" Joshua replied, tilting his head to the right as if he was surprised.

"Yeah, okay. I have to get to work now, so if you'll excuse me." Maggie pulled her arms close to her sides and inhaled as she slipped past Joshua, who barely made any attempt to get out of her way.

"Tomorrow is the café opening. I'm having it in late afternoon and early evening, so maybe some of the after-work traffic will slip in to get out of the rain," Joshua said.

"That's a good idea," Maggie said as she walked to the front of the store. When she turned around to ask Joshua another question, she collided right into him.

"I'm sorry." He chuckled.

"What are you following so close for?" Maggie snapped.

"I didn't know you were going to turn around." He shrugged.

"Yeah, well, ladies like Samantha Toonsley might like guys getting all up on them, but that doesn't mean we all do," Maggie blurted without thinking.

"What does that mean?" Joshua chuckled again.

"She came parading out of the back like she was marching off to war. And her bony son could use a few lessons in manners," Maggie said as she went to the display window. It was finished, but she didn't want to tell Joshua that yet. She would rather he see it when she wasn't there to hear any complaints or criticisms.

"Yeah, well, she wasn't very happy with me, I can tell you that," Joshua replied.

"Oh yeah? Why?" Maggie asked innocently.

"I wouldn't give her something she wanted."

"That doesn't sound too scandalous," Maggie chirped before pinching her lips together.

"No more scandalous than a pretty young girl who prefers the company of an old bookstore owner over anyone her own age." Joshua smirked at Maggie again.

"Very funny. Ha ha," Maggie replied and turned her back to him. She would have been mortified if he'd seen her blush after he called her pretty.

## Chapter 15

That day, rain or shine, Maggie had to take receipts and cash to the Old Cedar Bank. The Old Cedar Bank was a dignified building of brick, not cedar, but the lobby did incorporate some beautiful woodwork throughout. It made Maggie think of the Bailey Building and Loan in the short story *The Greatest Gift* by Philip Van Doren Stern. Most people knew the story by its movie name, *It's a Wonderful Life*.

The only thing Maggie didn't like about the place was that most of the women tellers were extremely chatty and asked a lot of questions. Maggie knew all of them but just hated to chitchat. Thankfully, as soon as she stepped into the lobby and folded her umbrella, she saw that Wilma DeForrest, the least talkative of the bunch, was free. Clutching her deposit bag in one hand and using the umbrella as a cane with the other, she hurried to Wilma's window.

"I'm depositing receipts and just a little over fifty dollars," Maggie said and wrinkled her nose as she pinched her eyebrows together.

"We haven't seen you in a while," Wilma said with a sly grin. She was an older woman who smelled strongly of

Opium perfume. It always reminded Maggie of an antique shop, except Wilma wasn't nearly that interesting. "How's work?"

"It's fine," Maggie replied. "Not the same without Mr. Whitfield."

"Oh, that's right. I'm sorry to hear of him passing," Wilma said almost like an afterthought. Maggie could tell by the way Wilma kept looking over her shoulder and smirking that something was going on. Maggie swallowed hard. She felt a conversation coming and wanted nothing to do with it.

"Could you hurry? I'd like to get back to the store before the rain picks up." She decided that was as good an excuse as anything.

"If I worked at the bookstore, I'd want to get back quickly too," Wilma whispered.

"What?" Maggie frowned at Wilma and waited for her to elaborate.

"You have to tell us what he's like," Wilma said.

A couple of the other tellers not tending customers came hurrying up to the window.

"What who's like?" Maggie tucked her hair behind her ear nervously.

"Mr. Whitfield's gorgeous son. Everyone is talking about the café opening tomorrow night. I wouldn't care if there was a tsunami. I'll be there for sure. We hear he's divorced. Is that true?" Wilma asked, and all three women leaned forward.

"I think so," Maggie said as she pushed the bag with the slips of paper and the deposit form toward Wilma.

"I heard he's under suspicion for Bo Logan's death," Joyce, one of the assistant managers at the bank, hissed from behind the cluster of ladies. "I'm not going anywhere near that place. It's bad luck."

"He's not under suspicion of anything," Maggie said. "We don't know what happened to Bo. There are some weird aspects of that whole night, but no one said Joshua did it."

"That's not what I heard," Joyce replied. She was tall, and her neck didn't go straight up from her spine. Instead, it jutted out as if she was continually trying to look over someone's shoulder. "I heard he's divorced and that he has a temper. Now, I'm not saying he killed anyone on purpose, but sometimes those people with hot heads can just snap and not even realize it."

Maggie looked Joyce up and down but said nothing. She didn't know if what Joyce was saying about Joshua having a temper was true. All she could say was that if he had a temper, he hadn't shown it to Maggie—and if she thought about it, she'd given him plenty of reason to put it on display. Plus, growing up with Alexander as his dad had to have been a peaceful upbringing.

"I heard that too. The police are keeping it hush-hush. Figures; all the good-looking men are either married or murderers," one of the other tellers replied.

Maggie looked down at the beautiful carvings on the umbrella handle and swallowed hard. She wanted to tell this group of clucking hens to shut their mouths. They didn't know Alexander Whitfield. And although Maggie didn't know Joshua all that well, she knew him better than they did. He was no killer. The fact that this was even being discussed by the bank employees, none of whom ever set foot in the bookshop, was a testament to the grapevine that ran through this town.

Wilma finished filling out the other side of the deposit forms, stamped them with the date, and handed it all back to Maggie. "We will see you tomorrow evening at the café. It ought to be fun," Wilma added.

Maggie just nodded and took her statement.

It was amazing how fast news travelled in Fair Haven. And Maggie had forgotten about the café opening even though they'd been planning for it since Joshua had arrived in town. It was why she'd had to get the display window finished. As she hurried back to the store, Maggie wondered why Joyce and the other women would say such things about Joshua right to her.

And who was spreading this rumor? It certainly wasn't Gary. He was a good policeman, and if he was investigating something, he would keep a lid on it until he had all the facts. Like that time a few summers ago when people had been complaining about street signs getting shot at. Everyone thought it was the Baylors' boy because he always bragged about his rifles and was at the gun range all the time and had a really bad haircut. But the culprit had turned out to be Rachael Sussex, a fifteen-year-old girl who was trying to impress a bunch of other girls by taking her parents' gun and shooting up some stop signs. Gary knew all along it wasn't the Baylor child and kept the secret to himself. What he had told Maggie was as true a statement as there had ever been.

"Have you ever known a teenage girl to keep a secret?" Gary had said to Maggie in confidence. "It didn't take long for her to give herself away. Sometimes, the best thing to do when trying to find out something is to sit still, be quiet, and listen to what's going on around you. That's the problem. People don't listen, Mags."

Gary had no idea how sage his advice was. But Maggie also knew that sometimes, when trying to find out something, a person might need to just insert themselves in the middle of it. She hated the idea of doing that. But when she saw Samantha Toonsley through the window of Spotlight Boutique, she thought it was fate. Samantha was holding half a dozen dresses by their hangers over her shoulder and was in a very deep conversation with the staff. Maggie had no idea why she decided to step inside, but she did.

Spotlight Boutique was a really fabulous space with exposed-brick walls and a hardwood floor that creaked a little when walked on. It smelled like a musky incense that wasn't too overpowering and gave the place a bohemian vibe. Thick wooden beams crisscrossed the ceiling. Mirrors on the walls were set in simple, elegant frames and went from floor to ceiling in order for the customers who could afford the clothing to see themselves completely.

The only downside to the place, in Maggie's opinion, was the clothes. They were pretty, yes. Very pretty. Very expensive. And Maggie thought they were as scandalous as Joshua's comment about his encounter with Samantha Toonsley. The blouses were always low cut. The skirts were always short and tight. The dresses left zero to the imagination. And it seemed the less fabric that was used, the more the item cost. But there was no denying that Spotlight Boutique was one of the gems of Fair Haven. It did an amazing business from what Maggie had heard, and the owner had been written up in several prestigious fashion magazines.

When Maggie crossed the threshold after folding her umbrella, she set off a tiny doorbell ping.

"Welcome to Spotlight," one of the ladies at the counter said without looking up.

Maggie nodded and proceeded to hide herself among the racks as she inched closer to where Samantha was standing. One thing Maggie was sure of: she wouldn't be noticed. She did not command attention when she walked into a room. It was both a gift and a curse. At times like this, it was a perfect quality to have. But there were other times when she would have liked a head or two to turn in her direction. Like when Joshua walked into the bookshop to get to the stairs to his father's apartment.

*Where did that thought come from?* Maggie shook her head and tried to focus.

Samantha didn't notice her, and neither did the two other women behind the counter, who were engrossed in conversation with the popular middle-aged cougar.

"I'm still going. There isn't an opening or ribbon cutting that Calvin and I would ever miss. But I've got my doubts. A new man arrives in town, and suddenly one of our own dies mysteriously? I'm not into conspiracy theories, but it is a little strange, don't you think?" Samantha said, her voice low, sultry, and almost hypnotic. It didn't take long for Maggie to realize where the rumors about Joshua were coming from.

Part of her wanted to march right up to Samantha and tell her she had seen their whole exchange in the alley and that Samantha was just mad because Joshua didn't fall for her babe-in-the-woods routine. But she kept her mouth shut and listened.

"Oh, come on, Sam. You can tell us. Is there something going on between you and Mr. Whitfield's son?" one of the salesladies asked. She was pretty, with long black hair pulled back and almond-shaped eyes, and she was as thin as a stick of dry spaghetti. But the question she'd asked made Maggie almost dry heave.

"No. My gosh, he's young enough to be my son," Samantha replied and giggled.

"Since when has that stopped you?" a saleswoman with round, knobby shoulders replied, making all of them giggle.

"True. He's got a few things to learn about how things are done here in Fair Haven," Samantha said. "And I'm just the one to teach them to him."

"What about Calvin? Isn't he ever suspicious?" the almond-eyed woman said.

"If he took time away from his big-busted secretary, maybe he would be. But we have a rather simple arrange-ment. He doesn't ask me what I'm spending, and I don't ask him who he's seeing. It works for us." Samantha laughed, making Maggie feel nauseous. "I will say this, though. It is an overwhelming aphrodisiac to know that the most handsome guy in town has something you want."

"You always did like the bad boys, Sam," Miss Knobby Shoulders said.

Maggie slunk back and forth between the dress racks.

Every so often, she looked down at a price tag to give the appearance that she was really shopping. When she saw one that read $160 for a plain white blouse, she squinted at the ticket again to make sure she was reading it right. Even if she'd had the money, she didn't dare think of spending it on clothes. She'd buy one of Mr. Whitfield's first editions.

"Yeah, and the bad boys like me. I spoke with Joshua Whitfield about making a trade. At first, he agreed," Samantha said. "Then he changed his mind after Bo dropped dead, like he knew there was something more there. He doesn't realize that I'm not afraid of him, whether he killed Bo or not. When I want something, I get it."

"So, speaking of getting things, would you like a fitting room for those?" the almond-eyed woman said.

"Oh, I almost forgot I had them. Yes. I need to look extra serious tomorrow night for the café opening. Joshua won't be able to hold out for too long. And when I'm done with him, I'll make sure the police know all about it," Samantha purred, making the other women laugh.

Maggie didn't know what to think. She could hardly get over the fact that a married woman well known in town so freely talked about having affairs and accepting her husband doing the same. But in addition, that Samantha would pass along a rumor about Bo's murderer being Joshua was a whole different level of gossipy. If Mrs. Peacock had heard half of what Maggie had just heard, she would be on the phone for hours, passing the information around.

But Maggie had no one to tell. There was no way she could believe such a thing about her new boss. He might have had terrible taste in books and no real knowledge of the classics, but that was hardly a crime. Sadly.

"You know that black dress you'd passed on is on sale. I know it's your size, Sam. Do you want me to grab it for you?" Miss Knobby Shoulders asked as she unlocked a fitting room for Samantha.

"No. If I can't pay full price, I don't buy it." Samantha laughed loudly, making the saleswoman laugh, too.

"Sam, you are too much." Miss Knobby Shoulders guffawed.

Maggie shook her head. What the heck kind of joke was that? There was nothing funny about a sale.

It didn't take long for Maggie to work her way through the store and finally end up close to the fitting room where Samantha was. The conversation between Samantha and Miss Knobby Shoulders shifted from Joshua to clothes, and Maggie quickly lost interest—until something on the sale rack caught her eye.

It hung from a hanger that appeared to be fancier than the dress itself. It was a simple red dress with an A-line skirt. It certainly was the most modest thing in the entire place and reminded Maggie of proms from the 1950s. She glanced over her shoulder to make sure no one was looking at her as she checked the price. It had been $170. Then it was marked down to $85. Now, in a last-ditch effort to sell the dress, it bore a final sale price of $60 and a handwritten warning that all sales were final and the dress was being sold as-is. Maggie inspected every inch of the dress, and aside from a bit of hem that looked to have come loose, it was in perfect condition.

It was the most she had paid for a dress in recent memory. Without hesitating, she snatched the dress from the rack, folded it in her arms, and hurried to the register. The woman with almond-shaped eyes gave a forced smile as she took the dress from Maggie.

"You do know that this is a sale dress and all sales are final?" she said. Her name tag read Shawna.

"I can read. Yes, I saw that," Maggie said, not meaning to be rude but just stating a fact. She pushed her glasses up and pulled her wallet from her purse, which was strapped across her body to leave her hands free.

Once Shawna rang up the dress and Maggie paid in cash,

she folded it nicely, wrapped it in tissue paper, stuck it in a pretty bag that had the image of a spotlight on it, and handed it to Maggie.

"Enjoy." Shawna again forced a smile that made her squint. ·

Maggie took the bag and, without a word, hurried out of the store. She was practically shaking as she hurried back to the bookshop. She didn't know what she was more excited about, the things she'd heard Samantha saying or the dress.

## Chapter 16

Despite the weather forecast predicting more steady rain and even a flash flood watch in some of the more rural areas, the people of Fair Haven were not deterred from an evening out. As she stood in front of the bathroom mirror and tried to get a look at herself in her new red dress, Maggie couldn't help feeling like she was playing a character in a book.

She'd never tell a soul, but she had taken the dress off three times after convincing herself it was too flashy, too scandalous, too red for the bookshop and café event. As she slipped it back over her head and adjusted her glasses for the fourth time, there was a knock on her door. Dropping her hands to her sides in frustration, she padded to the door in her bare feet and yanked it open with a fuss.

"Who the heck…oh, hello, Mrs. Peacock." Maggie tried to put on a smile as she pushed up her glasses.

"Why, Maggie, you look splendid!" Mrs. Peacock gushed.

"Oh, well, thank you, but I don't think I'm going to wear…" Maggie started but was quickly interrupted.

"Are you wearing that to the café tonight? Everyone in town is planning on stopping by. My goodness, I don't think

I've ever seen you look so dressed up. I do hope you aren't getting your hopes up for Joshua Whitfield." Mrs. Peacock frowned as the gossip hung there on the tip of her tongue, just waiting for the slightest nudge to fall out of her mouth.

"What?" Maggie crinkled her face and shook her head.

"I'm just looking out for you. I know how fond you were of Mr. Whitfield, but sometimes the apple falls far from the tree," Mrs. Peacock said from beneath her umbrella. "You know what everyone is saying about Joshua? That he had something to do with poor Bo's death. Now, I'm only saying what I heard."

"Mrs. Peacock, I don't think Joshua had anything to do with Bo's death," Maggie protested. "You can't tell me you really believe he did, too?"

"I'm not sure what to believe. That's why I'm going to the café to get a better look at him for myself," Mrs. Peacock replied.

"Was there something else you wanted? Or did you really just come *here* to tell me you were going *there*?"

"Oh, dear, I've plumb forgotten what I came to tell you. Well, I will tell you this: there isn't going to be a fellow in all of Fair Haven who isn't going to notice you in that dress. You look as pretty as a picture," Mrs. Peacock said. "You should dress up more often."

Maggie rolled her eyes as her landlady hurried back to the big house. She would probably be on the phone within seconds, telling someone in town about the scandalous red dress she was wearing.

When Maggie looked at the clock, she had zero time to change into one of her more sensible skirts and cardigan sweaters. She had no choice but to leave for the bookshop wearing what she had on. Without giving it another thought, she slipped into her black heels, grabbed the clutch purse that had three vintage rhinestone pins fastened to it, scooped up Mr. Whitfield's umbrella, and left. She'd promised Joshua she'd be there early in order to help with any last-minute details. She hoped he didn't expect her to do any touch-up painting or to polish any of the brass fixtures she'd seen him installing.

Thankfully, she found a parking spot just off the alley and took only a few steps before she was in the bookshop. Before she even pushed the door open, she smiled widely at the new lettering on it.

"The Bookish Café," she said before touching the bright-red letters with gold trim. It was a stunning replacement for the faded, chipped letters that had been on the door just a few days earlier. "Oh, Mr. Whitfield, you'd be so proud."

She walked in and quickly set her things deep beneath the counter so no one would see her purse or umbrella. Just as she was about to climb up into the display window and take down the sheets, a familiar voice came from behind her.

"Hello, Mags."

She turned and saw Toby. "Toby. I didn't know you were still in town," Maggie said.

"The bridges are still out. And now with those flash flood warnings, heaven knows when I'll be able to leave. But I have to say that of all the places to be stranded, I can think of none more quaint than Fair Haven. Although the streets of Bordeaux, France, will forever hold a special place in my heart," Toby replied with a sly look on his face.

"What were you doing in the back of the store?" Maggie asked.

"There was a specific book that I was looking for," Toby answered and looked down at the floor for a moment. "Alexander and I had had many discussions over it. Before he passed, he'd promised it to me. I was hoping that I might find it and take it with me on my journey back home."

"Was that *The Sound and the Fury*?" Maggie asked and narrowed her eyes.

"Yes." Toby smiled, his eyes twinkling.

"I don't have it," Maggie replied.

"What?" Toby's voice dropped to a low bass.

"Joshua told me I had to make room for the new books. So many of Mr. Whitfield's books were old, so I set them on a table for a quick sale. Some kid needed it for a book report. I sold it to him for fifty cents, I think. Maybe seventy-five." She smiled innocently.

"Surely you're joking," Toby said with a nervous smile.

"No," Maggie replied, knowing she wasn't joking, just lying to see what Toby would do. "I know Mr. Whitfield had some old books, and maybe they were worth a few dollars, but I also know that Mr. Whitfield was more interested in people reading the books, getting ideas and enjoyment from them, and that he would have given away everything if he thought it would make someone happy."

"You ignorant twit," Toby hissed.

"Hey!" was the only word Maggie managed to get out.

"That book was a signed first edition!" Toby shouted, making Maggie jump and take a step backward. "Do you have any idea what you've done? That book was my way out! It was worth over ten thousand dollars!"

Maggie straightened and squared her shoulders. "Is that so? Well, my customer paid cash. I have no idea who he was or where he went."

Toby took another step toward Maggie, his hands clenched into tight fists. His puffy jowls trembled with anger, and he ground his teeth together. "Alexander promised that book to me," he snarled.

"Upon receipt of payment in full. But you didn't have the money. You wanted him to just give it to you because you were friends. And when he wouldn't, you said the next time you'd see him would be at his funeral. How long have you been watching the obituaries, Tobias, waiting to see Alexander Whitfield's name listed? You're sick," Maggie hissed. Never in her life had she ever stood up to anyone this way. She was terrified.

"He promised me!" Toby shouted.

"You took advantage of Mr. Whitfield. And then you thought you'd come in here and steal his things. Did Bo Logan catch you? Is that why you flipped the fuse box for him to get electrocuted? Or did you accidentally kill him because you were trying to get rid of Joshua and anyone who had any legal claim to all these books?"

Maggie held her breath as she watched Toby's response. She couldn't say where her accusation of murder had come from. It had been tickling at the back of her mind, but she didn't want to think it was truly murder. An accident, maybe. But murder? She couldn't imagine it. But that didn't change the fact that people did kill for far less.

"I don't know what you are talking about. I wanted the book, but that was all. Mags, you don't know what I'm going through." Toby's whole body deflated like an inner tube slowly losing air. He smiled weakly. "I'm in trouble. I've gotten myself into a real pickle."

"Right. And Mr. Whitfield passing away has left *me* on the brink of no job and no prospects. But please, do go on about how hard you have it," she huffed, unaware of where that sarcasm had come from but enjoying it none the less.

"I'm in debt. If Alex had just given me that book, I would have been able to get out of it. I would have had a fresh start. Don't you see? I just needed his help. But I didn't kill anyone," Toby whimpered.

The sight of a man with Toby's worldly experience and his macho image starting to cry like a child made Maggie cringe.

"You didn't offer to buy it. You wanted him to just give it to you. And since he wouldn't, you were just going to steal it. If I hadn't seen the letter you wrote, I would never have believed it. Mr. Whitfield cared about you. And this is how you repaid him for his years of friendship." Maggie wondered how Mr. Whitfield had felt upon receiving the letter Toby had written him. If she had to guess, it had probably broken his heart. That brought tears to Maggie's eyes.

"I was sorry the minute I sent it," Toby replied as he looked at the ground.

"I'll be telling Officer Brookes what I know, and he'll be paying you a visit. No one is getting in or out of Fair Haven for the next three days while the rain continues. Of course, if you thought you could run and somehow get across the flooded bridges, I have the feeling you'd be joining Mr. Whitfield a lot sooner than you'd expected." Maggie pointed to the door.

"Mags...I really didn't hurt anyone. I could never hurt anyone," Toby said as he reached the door.

"That's a lie. You hurt Mr. Whitfield and thought nothing of it," Maggie hissed.

She watched as Toby stared at her sadly, swallowing hard before going out into the rain. For a moment, he was jostled by the other pedestrians hurrying past, but before long, he was out of sight.

Maggie's heart raced as she walked over to the display window. She barely saw the crowd of people who stopped to peek at the new display. Her mind was racing and frozen at the same time. Toby hadn't just behaved cruelly to Mr. Whitfield but had been ready and willing to take advantage of her too. It made her feel stupid. She folded up the sheets and tucked them away.

With all the excitement, she hadn't even noticed the beautiful shelves Joshua had put up on either side of the door that led to the café. They were simple yet elegant, and although she might not say it out loud, the way he'd set up everything up made even the contemporary romances and mysteries look enticing. She picked up a copy of *Manhattan Solstice* and turned it over to read the description aloud.

"My first wedding was in the fall, and it was beautiful until it wasn't. My second wedding took place in the summer, when the heat was there, but became unbearable. Now, in a new city with a new outlook, I've decided never to marry again. Unless the stars align and the moon is in its Manhattan Solstice…oh, gosh, those words just left the worst taste in my mouth." Maggie gagged. "I can't. Can't do it. Won't be reading this. I can't get those few seconds of my life back, nope, nope…"

She slipped the book back onto the shelf, smoothed her skirt, patted her hair into place as if the words she had read had somehow frazzled the strands loose from her bun, and adjusted her glasses.

Before she could mutter another word to herself, she heard someone behind her clear their throat.

## Chapter 17

"**W**ow," Joshua said as he looked at Maggie.

She had no idea that he had tried on two different shirts and three different ties before settling on what he was currently wearing. He had been nervous not just because there were rumors swirling around about Bo's death but because he was really afraid no one would come. He'd wanted to ask Margaret about the people of Fair Haven. According to his father, Maggie knew just about everyone by sight even if she never said a word to more than half of them. To the other half, she'd probably uttered only one word. But tonight, he didn't think she'd have a problem talking to anyone. She looked beautiful.

Maggie swallowed hard and cleared her throat. She almost said the same thing to him. Although she hadn't thought it was possible for him to look even better than he did in jeans and his tool belt, here he was in nice tan pants with a blue button-down shirt and tie, looking amazing.

"Hi, J-Joshua," Maggie stuttered. "Um, the bookshelf looks good. It really does."

"Margaret, you look so...different," Joshua said as he

stared. "I didn't know, I mean, I saw you in your slip the other night and didn't think you could look any prettier, but here…"

"What? No, I…uh…thank you. I think. Thanks, yes. Thank you," Maggie stuttered, putting her hand to her cheek and feeling the heat of embarrassment warming her palm. "You look very nice, too."

For someone who read and had a vocabulary like *Webster's Dictionary*, she knew she sounded like a dolt. Joshua was smiling at her obvious discomfort.

"You know, I looked at the back of this book, and it doesn't sound half bad," he said as if reading the back of *Manhattan Solstice* was a real accomplishment. But Maggie could tell he was trying to be nice.

"Well, if you read it, tell me if it's any good," Maggie replied, hoping he would drop it and maybe go back into the café. She was finding it hard to concentrate and not stare at his broad shoulders and strong, calloused hands.

"I'll do that." He smiled. "I was just about to open the café door, but I haven't seen the window yet and thought maybe I could get a look at…" He stopped speaking as he walked over to the display.

There was his father's highbacked chair with a coffee table in front of it. Maggie had attached some of the new books from wires, hanging them from the exposed pipes that were out of view from the outside window. Some of the older titles were stacked carefully along the floor with the titles facing the street. It looked like a cozy, magical place that was warm and welcoming and maybe just a little eccentric.

"What? You don't like it? Well, maybe next time. I've never decorated a window, and I thought that…" Maggie babbled more to herself than to Joshua.

"No. No, Maggie. It's amazing. I can't believe you did this." Joshua smiled when he turned around to face her. "My dad would have loved this."

Maggie didn't know why, but those words brought tears to her eyes. She smiled wide and shrugged.

"Come on." Joshua stepped down from the window display, grabbed Maggie by the hand, and pulled her into the café.

She'd intentionally avoided looking inside. She was afraid she'd like what she saw, and then she'd have to admit that Joshua's idea was a good one. Why that was a bitter pill to swallow she didn't know. But as he held her hand and she felt the calluses from all his hard work, a little guilt at how she'd treated him seeped in, especially after she saw how beautiful the place looked.

It was simple and elegant. No corny images of giant cups of coffee or Andy Warhol-style paintings of coffee beans. Instead, it looked as cozy and inviting as Mr. Whitfield's apartment just upstairs.

"So, what do you think?" Joshua asked.

"It looks…like your dad's place," Maggie replied with a wide smile. This time, it was Joshua's turn to have tears come.

"I miss him," Joshua replied.

"Me too." Maggie wanted to pat Joshua on the back, maybe even give him a hug. But instead, she continued to hold his hand until she noticed the cuckoo clock hanging on the wall. "Uh-oh. We better get things ready. We're supposed to open in fifteen minutes."

"Right." Joshua held Maggie's hand for a few seconds longer before looking down at her. "I think Tammy should be arriving any minute with some food."

"Okay. I'm going to go back to the bookshop side," Maggie replied.

"I might need your help here," he said softly.

"Oh, you never said that." Maggie nearly froze. The idea of being around people who were drinking and chatting and who might ask her questions about herself or anything at all made her breath catch in her throat.

"Well, I didn't think I had to," Joshua said.

"Sorry, I work in the bookshop. I don't work in a café. That's too much. Nope. I'll tend the bookshop," Maggie restated firmly.

"Margaret, now is no time to be stubborn," Joshua said.

"I'm not being stubborn. Stubborn would mean you told me what to do and I refused to do it. You never mentioned me working the café side, ever. So I can't be stubborn when I was never given an option. Perhaps you assumed too much. That's more like it," Maggie said with a serious face.

"You know, my father said you were peculiar," Joshua huffed.

"No, he didn't." Maggie put her hands on her hips.

"He did. He said you were pretty and smart and the most peculiar girl he'd ever met. Boy, was he right." Joshua shook his head.

"Well, he told me a few things about you too. But I'm not so rude as to repeat them. But you'd be shocked," Maggie replied before lifting her chin defiantly. She'd heard nothing but wonderful things about Joshua from his dad, but that didn't make his request any more acceptable.

Without giving him a chance to say anything more, she turned her back and hustled through the door that joined the two places. She'd made some plans of her own for the big event and walked over to a couple of antique side tables that had been covered with books for so long she was sure Mr. Whitfield had forgotten they were even there. With a little furniture polish she'd brought from home, she had cleaned them up and covered them so no one would see anything until the big unveiling.

She saw a couple people outside peeking in past her window display. She had no desire to make eye contact with anyone but instead busied herself with her additional displays of books.

It wasn't long before Maggie heard Tammy giggling and

chatting with Joshua in the café. Another fellow arrived with a couple cases of wine that Maggie heard clanking together as the white wines were thrust into a sink full of ice and the reds were lined along the counter. The smell of strong coffee brewing came into the bookshop, and soft classical music began to play over speakers Maggie hadn't even known had been installed.

It was as if the whole place was alive in a way it never had been before. Maggie thought of Mr. Whitfield and wished he could have been there with her. She could have sat with him, enjoying a cup of coffee and discussing another book or idea, while the world passed through the shop without noticing them. But she was quickly snapped out of her daydream.

"Oh, I've been dying to read this book!" Two women appeared in the doorway. One of them quickly snatched a copy of *Manhattan Solstice* from the shelves Joshua had made.

"Me too. I've heard it's really good."

Maggie slipped behind the counter. She took her seat on the barstool and waited for the ladies to finish perusing the store. They did purchase their books, and just as they left, another couple of people came in. They grabbed copies of *Autumn at Dawn* and some thriller titled *The Persistent*.

When she was alone, Maggie pulled out her copy of *The Streets of Laredo* and tried to read, but the bustle of customers was too distracting. It wasn't that she minded working; she didn't. But she hated the small talk and wished she could put up a sign that read *Please don't feed or talk to the staff*.

"Mags!" Officer Gary Brookes walked in, looking as sharp and official as always in his uniform. When he saw Maggie in her red dress with her hair up, he stopped for a minute and stared. After clearing his throat, he walked over to her.

"Hi, Gary," Maggie said as she handed the latest customer their book in a thin, crinkly brown paper bag.

"I never thought I'd see the day you had people in here,"

Gary said quietly as he leaned on the counter. "Are you doing okay?"

"I have no choice," she confided and wrinkled her nose as if she smelled something bad.

"You look really nice," Gary said. "And if I can give you some advice…"

"No, you can't," Maggie replied with a serious look on her face.

"Be yourself. You'd be surprised at how many people will think that's just fine." Gary winked. He stood up straight and was about to walk away when Maggie tugged at his sleeve.

"I need to talk to you about something," she said. When Gary smiled broadly with a twinkle in his eye, Maggie shook her head. "It's serious."

"Let me guess: Ruby Sinclair was at your house hopscotching on the square blocks of your sidewalk and tapping each porch lamp ten times." Gary smirked.

"Very funny! Gary, you're a hoot! Why aren't you married again?" Maggie pretended to laugh then became very serious as she told him about Toby. "He was in here, and he practically admitted he was here to take Mr. Whitfield's old books. I'm just letting you know. It's another person who might have been here when Bo was killed."

"What is this sudden interest in solving crimes?" Gary asked as he finished writing down the details of what Maggie had just said. "Are you trying to take an interest in what I do?"

"Are you nuts? I really don't have any interest in what you do. I'm just trying to be helpful." Maggie shook her head. She always could talk to Gary. Maybe it was because they had gone to high school together, or maybe it was because he looked so honest and brave in his uniform. Either way, he never seemed to be put off by her introverted nature.

"Okay, I'll go talk to Mr. Tobias Hodgkin. He's at the Scuccis' B&B?" Gary confirmed.

"If he hasn't tried to leave."

"He won't be going anywhere. It doesn't look like it's raining all that hard, but the bridges are about five feet underwater at the low ends. We've got patrol cars out there to make sure people turn around," Gary replied.

Maggie let out a deep breath and grimaced as more people came in from the café with plastic cups of red wine in their hands.

"If you spill that on a book, you've bought it." She pointed rudely.

The customers nodded and whispered to each other before turning around and going back into the café.

"That-a-girl. Way to make the customers feel at home," Gary teased.

"Hey, they could spill everything all over the books in the window. It's the classics that take up all the other shelves and tables that I'm worried about," Maggie huffed.

"Speaking of which, who did your window display? It's really cool. In fact, you're giving the beauty-supply store down the street a real run for their money. You know, there is always a window competition when the weather gets colder," Gary said as he started to walk back toward the café door.

"I did it," Maggie shouted back, a hint of a smile tickling at the corner of her mouth.

"I thought so. It looks like you," Gary replied. "Classy. Old-fashioned. Maybe a little mysterious." He winked before he left, making Maggie blush and twist her lips to the left side of her face.

Maggie had been enjoying herself as she listened to the music alone. As she studied the bookshop, she thought the place could use a good dusting and vacuuming. Mr. Whitfield's cubby had barely been cleaned out. There were more than twenty years' worth of papers and ledgers and things back there that Joshua had said to leave for the time being. If she cleaned that, there would be room for more books. She might be able to have a special place designated for the really old classics that were worth something. Keep them under lock and key. Maybe Joshua could build a better bookcase for them.

The thought of having him in the bookshop with her, hammering away and working up a sweat, was too much to contemplate. He'd probably want to chitchat, or he'd have that horrible construction-worker rock playing on the radio. She'd lose her mind.

"Why are you even thinking about him?" Maggie muttered to herself. "He's...not your type at all. You don't even know what your type is, but it isn't him."

Throughout the evening, Maggie couldn't get a single page read, because every time she settled into her book, she was distracted by customers who wanted to buy not just the bestsellers but some of the other books on the shelves. Maggie had had no idea that so many people in Fair Haven had an interest in books. Not just the classics but history and science and even a couple of old legal books that Mr. Whitfield had stashed on the shelves were on their way to new homes. Part of her felt a little guilty about how judgmental she'd been toward everyone. Of course, purchasing one book after a couple glasses of wine didn't make a person a dedicated bibliophile. Nor did it make Maggie want to rush right out and give everyone a hug for their support. But the experience made her feel she might have something to offer them if they were to come looking for another book in the future.

Just as she was feeling more comfortable in her own skin, Maggie heard the voice that she'd heard at Spotlight Boutique just a short while ago. Samantha Toonsley had arrived. Maggie could not remain in her seat and peeked casually around the bookcase Joshua had built leading into the café.

## Chapter 18

Peple were sitting on the eclectic furniture that made the space feel more like a clubhouse than a café. Everyone was smiling and talking, and small dainties of food were being passed around. The bartender was a young fellow who was chatting with Tammy as they both did what they could to keep up with the demand of people wanting refills of food and drink. Maggie stuck her neck a little too far out and was spotted by Wilma and the gang of tellers from the bank. She gasped when they squealed her name.

"We were wondering where you were," Wilma said as she hurried toward Maggie on the bookstore side of the business. All the women were still in their work clothes. But it was obvious they'd enjoyed a couple of drinks already. They were giggling and chatting like a flock of starlings. Wilma had taken her shoes off and was walking around in her nylons.

"I'm tending the bookshop. People are buying books, so I'm staying here," Maggie said as she pushed up her glasses and tried to back into her alcove of protection behind the small counter.

"We can't get over the place. It all looks so different. Well, the bookstore looks the same. But that café is amazing. You'd never know it was a dumpy abandoned building just a few weeks ago," Wilma said with a slight slur hanging on to the edge of her words. "And the murderer? He's as charming as ever. I only talked to him for a second. He's divorced, you know. His ex-wife will not be coming to the opening."

"Probably because of the weather," Maggie replied.

That answer hadn't crossed Wilma's mind. The way she looked at Maggie was as if she'd just told her that there was not only no more wine but she was cut off throughout all of Fair Haven.

"No. Probably because he was rough with her, or maybe he cheated on her. I'll bet he cheated. He looks like the kind of guy who could have a different woman every week," Wilma said, making the other women squeal at the juicy prospect.

"You don't know that. And you might want to keep your voice down. That's how rumors start. Joshua has enough on his plate," Maggie defended him.

"You certainly are defensive," Joyce snapped.

"He's my boss. I need this job. I don't think making things up benefits anyone involved," Maggie said. She looked around at the books, wishing one of them could jump off its shelf and offer some kind of rebuttal to these women.

"I didn't mean anything, Maggie." Wilma cleared her throat and managed to look sad. "I'm just having a good time. You are right. I won't say another word." She pretended to zip her lip and then lock it and throw away the key.

"Right," Maggie replied.

"And look at you. The building isn't the only thing to get a new look. I've never seen you all dressed up. You look amazing," Wilma said. The other women from the bank concurred, except for Joyce, who looked Maggie up and down before taking a sip of her wine and looking away.

"Thanks," Maggie replied and nervously smoothed out the front of her dress.

"Lucky no one thinks Joshua Whitfield looks like a killer," Joyce replied.

"Maybe they do, but who cares. He's not out to kill me." Wilma laughed, and the other tellers followed suit.

"He didn't kill anyone, Joyce," Maggie said quietly.

"Technically. But Gary Brookes told me that there were some new developments. You're not the only one who talks to the police, Maggie," Joyce snapped.

Maggie furrowed her brows and looked behind her as if the sharp retort and rude attitude had to have been directed at someone else named Maggie and not at her.

"Calm down, Joyce. Maggie isn't trying to steal Gary Brookes away from you," Wilma said, making Joyce glare at her and clench her jaw. "She saw Gary talking to you and nearly had a fit."

"I did not," Joyce snapped.

"Gary and I went to high school together. And we talk sometimes. I mean, two guys died in this place within the last couple of weeks. I sort of had to talk to him," Maggie muttered as she studied Joyce's expression.

Joyce continued to sip her wine and look in any direction but Maggie's.

"See, Joyce? I told you they were just friends," Wilma said and patted Joyce on the arm. "Besides, if Gary knew you were interested in him, he might pay a little more attention to you."

"Drop it, Wilma," Joyce hissed.

"I'm just saying that you sometimes have to lead that horse to water in order to make it drink," Wilma kept prattling on.

"I don't think I need your help, Wilma. Remember, I'm the manager at the bank. You are just a teller." Joyce huffed like a schoolyard bully.

All the other women gasped, but Wilma just shrugged and diverted her attention back to Maggie.

"You really do look pretty tonight. Have you talked with Josh?" Wilma asked.

"Of course. He's my boss. I sort of have to. Why don't you go talk to him?" Maggie urged, hoping the women would take the hint.

"We've been trying, but Samantha Toonsley has been at his side all night." Wilma sighed. "And you should see what she's wearing."

"What is she wearing?" Maggie asked. She'd had half a dozen dresses over her shoulder at Spotlight. Which one had she picked?

"Take a look." Wilma stepped aside for Maggie to peek around the corner.

Sure enough, Samantha Toonsley was talking with Joshua, who looked to be enjoying himself immensely as she flirted, smoothing out his collar and smiling at everything he said. She was wearing a black dress that was cut low in the front and hugged her hips before flaring out around her legs. Her heels were so high Maggie was sure she would get a nosebleed. There was no denying the woman looked amazing.

Maggie was no contest for that kind of display and quickly shrugged and pushed past the bank ladies in order to take her seat behind the counter. When she looked down at her dress to smooth it out, she felt a little bit silly for having thought she would ever get the attention of someone like Joshua. Sure, his father had always encouraged her to date, but he had been an old man. His eyesight had to have been going, and what else was he going to say? That was what old gentlemen did: they complimented young ladies and made them feel prettier than they really were.

"Are you ladies going to buy any books?" Maggie asked.

"Oh, I'm not much of a reader." Wilma shrugged and chuckled. "Unless you have some of those paperback romances with the ladies in slightly torn ball gowns in the arms of Fabio."

"I get all my books on Amazon," Joyce needled.

"Okay, then thanks for stopping by. You can go now."

Maggie cleared her throat nervously and began to shuffle some of the paper bags in an attempt to look busy.

Just then, Poe hopped up on the counter, stretched out lazily, and let Maggie stroke his coat.

"I want to keep the register area open for paying customers. But why don't you look around. Maybe you'll see something that looks interesting. Harlequin Romance novels are in the back corner, across from the westerns." Maggie pointed.

"I could use another drink," Joyce suggested, to which the other bank ladies agreed. Before Maggie could say anything else, they were bustling back toward the café without another word in her direction.

"Or maybe not," Maggie huffed as they went back into the café, toward the soft lighting and the smell of strong coffee and pretty music, which had gone from classical to smooth jazz. With half the town of Fair Haven meandering back and forth, Maggie missed Mr. Whitfield more than ever. He had been her friend—her only friend—and she wished he was here. He would have enjoyed the party, and he would have enjoyed the people, even if Maggie shied away from every one of them.

Still, she was shocked at how many people did come into the bookshop, who did seriously look around, and who did buy something. What was even more astonishing was how many of them knew her name and spoke kindly of Mr. Whitfield. She had been sure he'd never left the bookshop. She'd always found him in roughly the same place every day when she came to work, sitting in his cubby or roaming the aisles of books for something new to read or something old to reread. When had he met everyone?

"Mr. Whitfield will be missed this year. We'll have to find a new Santa Claus," one woman who worked with special-needs kids said to Maggie, making her gasp.

"He played Santa?"

"Every year for the past ten years," the older woman said.

The book club ladies came by and gushed all over Maggie's new dress.

"Have you ever thought of contacts, Maggie? You've got such pretty eyes. Not that your glasses don't suit you. They do. But for a change of pace, a different look," Mrs. Pine suggested with a kind, wrinkly smile.

"I do, but I'm too squeamish to wear them," Maggie replied and pushed her glasses up on her nose.

"We miss Alexander. We don't know who is going to recommend our books from now on," Mrs. Lennox added.

"He suggested your books for your book club?" Maggie asked. "I never knew."

"Oh, yes. And I don't think we were ever disappointed with one of his suggestions. He was such an eclectic man. Well rounded. For a man who never left Fair Haven, he was more knowledgeable than any teacher at the community college."

Maggie was shocked at all the people who had known Mr. Whitfield. But perhaps the most shocking was Tammy from the bakery. When she stopped by, Maggie thought for sure she was going to burst into tears.

"Maggie, I almost didn't recognize you," she said sweetly.

"Hi, Tammy." Maggie took a deep breath and smoothed out her skirt for the hundredth time.

"Alexander would be so proud if he could see you right now. You know he loved you like his own daughter," Tammy replied.

"Thank you, Tammy."

"You know, he and I talked a great deal about you when he came to the bakery. He worried that you were staying close by because of him. That you might not see in yourself what he saw if he didn't let you go eventually." Tammy put her hands together.

"Oh, he didn't have to worry about me," Maggie said. "I like being alone."

"I do too sometimes." Tammy smiled. "But sometimes that can lead to being lonely."

"Sometimes," Maggie whispered.

"If you ever feel that way, honey, you come and see me. Any time. Day or night. Okay?" Tammy patted Maggie's hand.

"Okay," Maggie said. She'd never admit, even to herself, that sometimes she did feel lonely. Sometimes. And she'd never whisper to a soul that with Mr. Whitfield gone, she was terribly sad. She worried about her future and what was going to happen as she crept toward middle age. Although she had some savings because her rent was cheap, she hardly had a nest egg. She shook her head to scatter the negative thoughts away and smiled at Tammy.

"I have to say the bookstore looks beautiful. And who did the window?" Tammy asked.

"I did," Maggie said, her back straightening with pride.

"Oh, the beauty salon is not going to be happy. Looks like there will be some serious competition this year during the winter festival. See, that's what Alexander knew about you." Tammy smiled and smoothed a few wisps of Maggie's hair away from her face. "He knew you had more to offer than you were letting on."

After Tammy went back to the café, Maggie walked over and looked at her window display. There were people on the other side admiring it as well. They waved to her, and she waved back before they went on their way. She rocked on her heels and felt proud of herself.

Finally, it sounded as if the evening was wrapping up. People continued to sweep through the bookshop, commenting on the beautiful display window while making a serious dent in the inventory of new books. Many of the older books were still in their places, and Maggie was glad for that. There were still so many she hadn't read. But as she rang up the last person buying a copy of *Manhattan Solstice*, she was shocked to see the cash and credit card receipts in the till.

When Maggie stepped around the counter and went to lock the bookshop door, she couldn't help but hear a few people still talking in the café. She saw Calvin Toonsley chatting about the stock market and looking at his Rolex in front of a doe-eyed woman wearing no wedding ring.

Meanwhile, Joshua and Samantha were nowhere to be seen. Maggie took a deep breath before suddenly realizing her feet were aching in her heels. She rarely wore shoes like this, but she didn't want anyone to see her take them off and walk around barefoot. Since no one was coming to the bookshop side at this point in the evening, Maggie walked down the aisle and slipped out of her shoes. She wiggled her toes against the cool, aged hardwood floor.

Just then, Joshua appeared, and he was looking around. Just as Maggie was about to make her presence known, Samantha showed up again.

"You didn't think I was going to give up that easily, did you?" she purred.

"You haven't given up all night. Samantha, your husband is just across that threshold, and I think he's had more than a few glasses of wine," Joshua said.

"Look, I donate to a lot of powerful people in this town. I'm invited to every fundraiser, everyone knows me, and if I were to say that you did something not so nice, well, you can bet that this little business of yours would be shut down before you can say Ernest Hemingway," she hissed.

"Are you threatening me, Samantha?" Joshua asked.

Maggie stood perfectly still and watched from between the bookshelves. Neither Joshua nor Samantha knew she was there.

"Yes, I am," she hissed.

"I'm sorry, but I'm not interested in doing any business with you under these circumstances," Joshua replied.

"I gave you a chance. You'll be sorry," Samantha said before flipping her hair and stomping out of the bookshop.

Maggie took a step toward him and was about to reveal herself when Tammy appeared. "It looks like that's the end, Josh. Everyone is clearing out. And I think the bartender wants to get paid," she whispered.

"Oh, yeah. I've got his cash for him. Thanks, Tammy. Everything was wonderful," he said as they walked back into the café.

Maggie thought she'd wait for him to come back but decided that might take a while. There was nothing to be done with the cash in the register that couldn't wait until morning. Replenishing the display shelves could also wait until morning. So Maggie decided she would slip out unnoticed.

As she pulled the door to the bookshop closed behind her, locking it from the outside and then opening her umbrella, she didn't notice the slouching form that was waiting in the shadows.

## Chapter 19

**M**aggie hopped into her car and drove home. The rain had continued all evening. Maggie wondered how many sales there would have been had the weather been a little more accommodating. She started to compare how many people had shown up with the total number of people in town and an estimate of how many actually read books. Well, it wasn't a scientific formula, but she felt a twinge of excitement at the prospect of nicer weather meaning more sales. That would ensure Mr. Whitfield wouldn't be forgotten in Fair Haven.

As she let herself into her house, she was feeling something she hadn't felt in a long time: excitement. She was excited that so many people had come into the store. She hadn't liked talking to any of them, but she had done it anyway. And no one had screamed in horror or pointed at her as if she had suddenly sprouted a second head. In fact, no one had really seemed to notice how nervous she was. That was exciting too.

*And Joshua noticed you too*, she thought.

"Oh, no. That was nothing. He was caught up in the

excitement of the night," she said. She kicked off her shoes with a groan of relief and walked to the bathroom to get undressed. Before she could put her pajamas on, there was a knock at the door.

"Mrs. Peacock, what do you want now?" Maggie muttered. Without thinking, and breaking one of her own basic rules, she opened the door without the chain in place.

"How was the party?" Roger Hawes snapped. He had clearly followed Maggie home.

She let out a yelp then squinted to focus on the man's shiny, wet face. "Roger Hawes? What are you doing here?" Maggie gulped and partially hid behind the door as if she were not dressed. She could see that his wrinkled clothes were sticking to him.

"I need to talk to you." He wiped off his face with his pudgy hand. "You're in a lot of danger. You've got to listen to me."

"Roger, have you been drinking?" Maggie pursed her lips and narrowed her eyes.

"You always seemed like a nice girl. A little weird but decent enough."

"You have been drinking," Maggie muttered.

"No, I haven't. But I wouldn't mind a little snort of whiskey at the moment. Can I come in? You wouldn't happen to have a…"

"No, Roger!" Maggie stated and rolled her eyes as she closed the door so just her face showed. "Can you get to the point?"

"Mr. Whitfield was not that close to his son for a reason," Roger said.

"I think you should go home, Roger. Would you like me to call you a cab?" Maggie said as she went to shut the door.

Roger slapped his meaty hand against it to keep her from shutting it all the way. "You know he killed Bo Logan. He did that because he took out a new insurance policy on the men working for him. He's going to be a very rich man when that insurance policy pays out," Roger said, his cheeks red as if the strain of holding the door open was the most exercise he'd gotten in a decade.

"I don't know anything about his insurance. I don't know how you do either," Maggie replied. She'd had more than enough confrontations today. All she wanted was to get into her pajamas and finish reading her book.

"I know people, Maggie. And I know that Joshua Whitfield is a hack carpenter. He uses bad materials. He's got more than one creditor out to get him. You know he is responsible for Bo's death. You know he is. And what's more, he doesn't care. He won't care when something bad happens to you," Roger said.

"What do you mean by that?" Maggie stared at Roger through the crack in the door.

"Like I said, you seem like a nice girl. I'm just looking out for you," Roger said and clumsily cracked a smile as if it was something he wasn't accustomed to doing. His face looked as if it had been bisected with a broken piece of porcelain.

Roger Hawes had never looked out for anyone other than Roger Hawes. There was something going on, and Maggie didn't like the sound of it. Roger was up to something.

"I think it's time you leave, Roger. Don't make me call Gary Brookes to come and escort you off the property. Or worse, Mrs. Peacock herself," she said.

At the mention of the lady of the estate, Roger's face went gaunt, and he looked over his shoulder. It wasn't as if Mrs. Peacock had a black belt in karate or even a twelve-gauge shotgun to protect herself. What she did have was the fastest-dialing fingers on the East Coast, and Roger knew if the word got out that he had been lurking around the property to harass Mrs. Peacock's tenant, well, Roger Hawes might have his own problems getting work in Fair Haven. He was known as an extreme cheapskate himself, and the last thing he needed was to have the rumor floating around that he had come to bully the quietest, shyest woman in town.

"You just be careful, Maggie. Things happen when you least expect them," Roger said as lightning flashed and a low growl of thunder rumbled.

Maggie watched him back off the porch, pull his soaked collar up around his neck, and hurry down the sidewalk, past the big house, and into the darkness. She shut the door and slipped the lock into place, leaning against the door.

"I can't call Gary and tell him he needs to look into Roger Hawes, too," she said to herself. "I told him I suspected Ruby Sinclair, then Toby, and now Roger is showing up at my house in the rain with cryptic warnings."

Maggie thought for a moment.

When she finally made up her mind, she walked to her room, pulling off her dress at the same time, and grabbed a pair of sweatpants and a baggy flannel shirt. Without any thought, she let her hair fall to her shoulders and dashed out the door with her umbrella and car keys. It didn't take her long to get to the bookstore, which was now dark and quiet.

"I'll tell Joshua what he said and then be on my way. That way he can deal with Roger or not. I've done all I can. I feel like I'm babysitting," she muttered to herself as she parked the car in front of the bookshop.

When she got out of the car and looked up, she saw just a slight glow of light from the upstairs apartment.

Maggie took a deep breath and walked to the door. After collapsing the umbrella, she unlocked the door quickly, as she was getting wetter by the second. The rain wasn't pouring down; it was just constant. Maggie usually enjoyed rainy days better than sunny ones. There was something about the sound of it against the windows that encouraged snuggling under blankets or wrapping up in a bulky sweater with a good book.

Suddenly, the idea of cozying up under a thick blanket with Joshua Whitfield popped into her head, making her hands tremble.

"What are you, crazy?" she whispered as the deadbolt slipped back with a loud click.

Maggie stepped inside, closing the door gently behind her. The smell of coffee lingered just below the scent of all the books she'd surrounded herself with for so many years. When she thought back over the years she'd worked with Mr. Whitfield, she couldn't recall a time she'd ever been required to come to the bookshop when it was this dark and late in the evening.

A shiver suddenly ran up her spine. Maggie, who prided herself on reading books of all genres, suddenly found herself recalling scenes from some of the scariest titles she'd read. The faint triangles of light cast through the display window by the streetlamp down at the end of the block offered her no comfort.

"You're being silly," she whispered. "This place is the same now as it was this morning. Get a hold of yourself."

She propped her umbrella by the door so she wouldn't forget it and proceeded to walk into the store that she knew so well. Books no longer lay on the floor beside the counter, since she'd moved them for the event. The coffee-table books that had been sticking out had also found a new home, where they could be seen without snagging someone's leg or skirt, so the aisle to the back staircase was clear.

Except it wasn't.

Maggie carefully walked to the back of the store, running her fingers gently along the spines in the bookcase on her right to keep herself from getting scared. This was Mr. Whitfield's shop. These books held some of the greatest stories ever told. They'd been her friends for years. There was nothing scary here.

But just as she was about to let out the breath she was

holding, Maggie's foot snagged on a book on the floor. As if that wasn't bad enough, she kicked and stumbled over another then tripped completely over a stack of books that had been left on the floor, and she landed with a thud on her face.

"What in the world?" She looked behind her, knowing she hadn't left any books on the floor, and was sure that none of the visitors had been so rude as to leave a random stack lying around. Where had they come from? Oh, what she was going to say to Joshua for messing with her things!

She let out a long sigh as she pushed herself up to her knees, careful not to use any books on the shelves as her support lest she find herself back on the floor.

As she was about to get to her feet and call out for Joshua, she saw something. Between the books and through the shelving units, Maggie looked into the darkness of the shop. With her mouth hanging open, she watched as a pitch-black shadow shifted in the far corner of the room.

It was a trick of the light. Her eyes hadn't adjusted properly. When she'd fallen, she'd just gotten a little more shaken up than she'd thought. But if that was the case, she couldn't understand why her body just didn't want to move. She strained her eyes, sure that she'd eventually see what was really moving back there. But as she looked even harder, she was sure she saw someone standing there.

*No, no one is in the store now. Joshua had the door locked. Nobody would be here.* Maggie tried to calm herself, but her hands had become slick with sweat, and her heart was pounding.

Before she could scream, she heard the purr of a cat. Poe.

"Of course." Maggie let out a deep breath and sank onto her haunches with relief. It was Poe she'd seen move. In the darkness, his shadow had looked bigger than it really was. That was all. It was just the silly cat.

Maggie shook her head and began to stand up but stopped again as Poe slunk around her legs and took a seat on one of the open pages of the books there. When Maggie looked to the corner again, it looked different, as if something had moved from its hiding place. Something a lot bigger than the cat.

Just then, she saw something else move out of the corner of her eye.

When she turned, a huge shadow came lumbering toward her.

Without thinking, Maggie scurried over the books on the floor and ran into the maze of shelves, hoping to hide herself in a shadow.

"Joshua? Is that you?" she shouted, hoping maybe he'd think she was a burglar or trespasser or something. But there was no answer.

Maggie hurried to the western section. It was set in a zigzag sort of pattern. If a person didn't know, they'd collide with the shelves, giving themselves away. Carefully, she held onto the shelves on either side as if she might at any minute fall to the ground.

Her senses were on hyperalert. Every creak or groan of the floor sounded like a shrill car alarm. Where was Joshua? Someone was upstairs; she had seen the light.

As she inched her way through the western section of the shop to the almanacs and reference section, she was suddenly struck with a strange scent. It was so strong it left a soapy taste in her mouth. Before she could stop herself, a sneeze raced from her eyes down her nasal passages.

"A-choo!" she gasped.

She held her breath, stretched her eyes wide open, and listened. In front of her, a form appeared. Darker than even the darkest shadow, it stood taller than Maggie as it approached. Without hesitating, Maggie began to grab the books from the shelves and throw them at the thing as it slowly approached. She ran around the nearest bookcase, pulling down books behind her to trip up her attacker. It worked just enough for her to see the front door and safety outside in the rain and inside her locked car. But before she realized it, the phantom shape was no longer behind her but appeared in front of her.

Maggie screamed. She swiftly turned and made a mad dash to the staircase to the upstairs apartment. She was going to kill Joshua if he'd been sleeping through all of this.

But just before she made it to the steps there was a loud cry, the yowl of a cat, the cascade of at least a dozen books from the shelves, and finally, a loud thud. Maggie stood as if her feet had turned to stone. She waited but heard nothing. Without waiting for something else to come after her, she bolted up the stairs and burst into Joshua's apartment.

He was lying on the floor. His shoes were off, and he was in his stocking feet, wearing plaid pajama bottoms and no shirt.

Maggie wasn't sure what was more alarming—that he was lying there on the floor or that he was bare-chested. She swallowed hard, but there was practically no spit in her mouth. Within seconds, she was at his side, trying to shake him awake without touching his bare skin. But pushing his legs didn't seem to be doing the trick.

"Joshua? Joshua! Wake up! Wake up!" she said, finally mustering up enough courage to tap his cheeks and push his hair back on his head. He was so handsome. And he smelled of a spicy, soft cologne that was nothing like the toxic fumes she'd inhaled downstairs. Where had she smelled that before? Maggie felt the answer on the tip of her tongue when Joshua groaned.

"Oh, thank goodness. Joshua! Joshua! Someone is downstairs in the shop! Joshua! Oh, please wake up," Maggie muttered as she leaned over him to look down on his face.

Finally, his eyes popped open, and he blinked for a minute. She said nothing as he looked at her, and a smile crept over his lips. He reached up slowly and touched the side of her face, pushing her hair aside gently.

"Margaret, you look so pretty," he whispered.

"What? Oh, uh, yeah, thanks," she stuttered and smiled, wishing she could enjoy the moment and see where it might take her. But the thought of the shadow downstairs was like a bucket of ice water over everything. "You need to snap out of it. Joshua? Are you all right?"

"Oh, my head," he groaned.

"What happened to you?" Maggie asked as she helped Joshua sit up.

"I don't know. I came out of the bathroom and was getting ready to go to bed, and the next thing I know, you're here." He reached up and touched the back of his head. "I think maybe there was some kind of gas leak, or maybe I had a reaction to some fumes from something. I remember smelling some weird lemony scent that was…wow…strong."

"I smelled that too. But it isn't a gas leak. It's cologne. Or perfume," Maggie gasped.

But before she could put the face to the scent, there was a creak on the stairs. Both of them looked to the darkness. Maggie moved first, prompted by fear, and tried to shut the door, only to see a black-gloved hand and arm thrust through the opening.

She screamed and tried to run to Joshua and get him to his feet. The only light in the apartment was the rotating glow from the fireplace. It made Maggie feel as if she was in a carnival funhouse with a homicidal carny chasing her down.

"What do you want?" Joshua shouted as the shape pushed the door open and grabbed Maggie before she could get away.

"I want the book," the man said, holding her tightly by the wrist.

Maggie's body went rigid as she felt a deep affection for each and every tome Mr. Whitfield had collected and shared with her. Of course, there was a shiny blade in the man's other hand that also made her freeze.

"Which one? Let her go, and you can take any book you want," Joshua shouted.

"I want the one Samantha Toonsley wanted," the man said as he jerked Maggie in front of him and slipped his arm around her waist. He stuck his head over her shoulder, and she felt the scratchy texture of the black ski mask over his face. No wonder he had looked even darker than the shadows downstairs.

"What the heck book is that?" Joshua barked.

"*Sierra Madre Heights*, idiot!" the man shouted.

Maggie felt a shiver run up her spine when he shouted and was almost ready to gag from the smell of his cologne. It was what had made her sneeze downstairs. And it was the same smell that had made her react the day she saw Joshua in the alley with Samantha Toonsley.

"Heath?" Maggie managed to squeak out the name.

"Shut up!" he shouted and jerked Maggie violently against him. "This isn't a game!"

"You can't have it," Joshua replied coldly.

"I'm telling you right now, I want that book!" the man screamed.

"Heath Toonsley?" Maggie queried.

"Shut up!" he barked in her ear, making her shake and lift her hands up helplessly.

"All right," Joshua said as he put his hands up in the surrender pose. "But the book is downstairs, and you have to let her go before I'll give it to you."

"Fat chance, pal! Now get the book, and she won't get hurt," the ski-masked intruder said.

As Maggie thought back to the day she had seen Heath in the store, she didn't recall anything exceptional about him. He had been rude, and she stuck by her initial thought that someone needed to teach him some manners.

Maggie could tell by the look on Joshua's face that he wasn't planning on just going along with being ordered around by a masked marauder. Something was churning into a plan in his head.

The intruder must have sensed it too, because he yanked her aside for Joshua to go down the stairs first. The blade he held flashed in the golden light of the fireplace.

## Chapter 20

As they made their way downstairs, Maggie wished someone would say something. Instead, it was a twisted procession to the main floor. Every creak of the floor, the sound of the wind picking up and throwing the rain into the windows, and Maggie's own heartbeat thundered in her ears.

"Get the book," the man ordered.

"What book is it again?" Joshua asked weakly.

"*Sierra Madre Heights!*" the man shouted, making Maggie jump.

Joshua's shoulders slumped with defeat as he walked helplessly toward the back of the store.

Maggie knew exactly where *Sierra Madre Heights* was located. It was a thick book in hardback. The color had faded from a rich pine to cooler green, with the design and lettering on the cover and spine in a chipped and fading navy blue. The pages had yellowed beautifully, and there wasn't a single pencil mark or bent corner on any of them. It was in what a collector would call excellent condition and would fetch a very pretty penny. Maggie was sure it was worth at least fifteen thousand dollars to any serious collector. Why Heath—or whoever this was—wanted this book and was willing to kill for it Maggie had no idea.

Joshua held up the book in one strong hand then pointed at Maggie with the other.

"Let her go, and you can have your book," he said. Even though it was nearly pitch black in the store Maggie was sure Joshua's teeth were clenched in anger. Lightning flashed outside. The rain was still steadily coming down.

"Put the book on the counter," he ordered and squeezed Maggie again around the waist as if to remind both of them it wouldn't take much for him to hurt her if he had to.

Joshua did as he was told. Just then Poe, not knowing this was no time for a kitty to make himself known, hopped silently up onto the flat surface and scared Maggie's captor.

"What the…!" he shouted.

His grip loosened just enough for Maggie to slip to the ground. Without hesitating, she crawled like a crab into the shadows of the bookcase. But instead of trying to hide, she pushed as many books as she could off the shelves and onto their intruder. A few yelps of shock and pain assured her she'd hit her target.

Within seconds of chaos breaking out in the store, Maggie saw through the empty shelves that Joshua was also throwing books at the man. But it was of no use. He wouldn't drop his knife. He scooped the book up in one arm and, while brandishing the weapon in the other, stumbled and staggered across the store, trying not to trip over all the books on the floor and fall on his own blade.

Maggie was furious. He was getting closer and closer to the door! In just a few more seconds, a few more steps, he'd be out of the shop with Mr. Whitfield's book. It was a first edition. They'd read that book together.

"Stop him!" Maggie shouted.

Joshua was too far behind, having stood still for fear that the man might hurt Maggie in the process of trying to escape.

As the masked man heard Maggie shout, he moved faster, slipping on the uneven piles of books she'd pushed on top of him. Like a drunken sailor trying to stay on his feet as his ship tossed and turned on the ocean, the intruder lost his balance and slammed into the door with a loud grunt. Before Maggie could think of anything else, he'd yanked the door open and dashed out into the night.

"He'll never get top dollar now if the book gets wet," Maggie huffed.

"Are you all right?" Joshua asked.

"Yeah. But your dad's book. It was a…" Maggie looked up at Joshua. In the faint light from the streetlamp. "Your head. You got clunked on the noggin. We better call an ambulance along with the cops."

"I'm all right. Are you?" Joshua asked.

"Yeah, I'm fine," Maggie huffed. "Just had a knife pointed to my gut for the past five minutes, but other than that, yeah, I'm just ducky."

"What are you doing here?" Joshua said before he snapped the lights on.

"What am I doing here?" Maggie stopped for a minute. With all the excitement, she'd forgotten why she had even come back to the bookstore.

"You didn't have anything to do with that, did you?" Joshua asked and stared at her for a moment, blinking as the thought that she might have had something to do with the robbery floated past his eyes.

"Are you serious?" she snapped.

"I don't know. It just seems like a very strange coincidence that you arrived right after I was hit on the head," Joshua stated.

"Huh! If I hadn't arrived, you'd be lying upstairs on the floor, and that guy would have probably left with half the store." Maggie frowned. "Of course, he wouldn't have gotten

134

much for the new stuff you bought." She waved her arm at the shelves with copies of *Manhattan Solstice* on them.

"Hey, you saw how many people bought that stuff this evening. I wasn't wrong to invest in that," Joshua snapped.

"No, and I'm sure that Samantha Toonsley will be begging to know what the next book you recommend will be," Maggie said then instantly bit her lip. She was glad they were still in the dark, because she would have been mortified if he saw her cheeks flaming red with embarrassment at giving herself away.

"I wonder why that jerk wanted the same book she did," Joshua mused.

"That was her son," Maggie replied as she hurried to what had been Mr. Whitfield's cubby and picked up the phone.

"What? What are you doing?" Joshua put his hands on his hips. With the phone to her ear, Maggie shrugged at him. It was almost impossible for her not to notice his near nakedness, but she managed to keep her eyes locked with his and not on his pectorals.

"I'm calling the police," Maggie said.

"This is my store. I should be the one calling the police," he snapped.

"Fine, call the police," she replied with an eye roll.

"Fine, give me the phone."

"It's right here," Maggie huffed and set the receiver on the desk before walking away with her arms folded over her chest. She listened as Joshua told the 9-1-1 operator what had happened. As soon as he hung up, she walked over to the piles of books that she'd pushed off the shelves and started to pick them up.

"What are you doing?" Joshua asked as he took a seat on the stool that was hers when she sat behind the counter.

"Cleaning up. What does it look like?"

"Maybe we should leave everything for the police to see," he said.

"But we made this mess. It isn't like the perp would have left his fingerprints on it," Maggie replied.

"We? I think *you* made that mess," Joshua teased.

Maggie hated when he acted cute like this. It was almost impossible for her not to smile. She bit the inside of her lip and continued picking up the books.

"If I hadn't made this mess, heaven knows what that little twerp would have done."

"So are you saying you saved the day?"

"If the shoe fits," Maggie huffed. But just as she was about to turn around and give Joshua a real piece of her mind, she stopped and stared at the carpet.

"What's the matter?" Joshua asked. "Maggie? Are you okay?"

"He's been stabbed," Maggie replied.

When she stood up, her whole face had gone white. Joshua watched as her eyes rolled upward. Before she could fall and possibly hit her head, Joshua was off the stool and had her in his arms.

This had to be what all those people who claimed to have been abducted by aliens meant when they spoke of lost time. Maggie saw nothing but black and a tiny pinpoint of light way off in the distance.

"Maggie? Maggie, wake up. Say something."

She heard the voice but couldn't place who it was. As she focused on the little point of light, she felt like she was swimming, paddling madly for it. Slowly, it began to get bigger and brighter until she could see it was Joshua calling her name, and she was in the bookstore, looking up at the ceiling. Why was she looking up at the ceiling? What was she even doing there? Had she collapsed at the café opening? Oh, the rumors and the humiliation! Everyone would think she was drunk and…

"Maggie? Are you all right?"

"What happened?" she asked, wrinkling her nose.

"You saw blood and fainted," Joshua said.

"I didn't get drunk at the café opening?" She twisted her mouth to the side.

"No." Joshua chuckled.

"Oh, my gosh. This is embarrassing." Maggie tried to push herself up.

"Don't be in such a hurry. I've got you," Joshua said.

"I'm okay," Maggie lied. She would have lain in Joshua's arms until the Rapture if she thought she could, but the last thing she wanted him to think was that she had some kind of schoolgirl crush on him. Especially when half the female population seemed to be interested in the old bookseller's son.

"The police are on their way. An ambulance will be with them. We'll have you checked out," Joshua said. He tried to get Maggie to remain still to no avail.

"You're the one who got knocked out," Maggie replied. She quickly scrambled away from Joshua as if he had cooties. "You're the one who needs your head examined."

"Very funny. Head examined. Can't you ever just say yes to what I'm telling you to do?"

"If what you told me to do made any sense."

"I really don't know what my father saw in you." Joshua shook his head as he got to his feet. "And who faints at the sight of blood these days?"

Maggie's eyes bugged out as she looked around the floor. "That wasn't my blood. And I don't think it was your blood. That means that Heath Toonsley stabbed himself."

"How do you know it was Heath Toonsley? And who is Heath Toonsley?" Joshua asked.

"How many Toonsleys do you know? You obviously know Samantha." Again, the words just sort of tumbled out of Maggie's mouth before she could stop them.

"Yes, I know Samantha, and I know her husband. So what is your point?"

"They have a son, Heath. He wears a cologne that makes

my eyes burn. That's what I smelled when he got close to me. I think he's the one who stole your book," Maggie said. "But I can't imagine he stole it for his mother. That would be a little suspicious, with her pestering you for it over and over and then it suddenly coming up stolen. That doesn't make any sense."

Just then, the red and blue lights cut through the darkness, illuminating the inside of the bookshop.

"That's if it was him," Joshua said as he walked to the door to hold it open for the police officers.

"Yikes. If it wasn't, that means there is another person parading around unaware they smell like lemons dunked in Pine Sol," Maggie huffed.

"Okay, Sherlock. Sounds like you solved the case," Joshua replied as he gave the approaching officers a wave.

Maggie stuck her tongue out at him just as Gary Brookes walked in.

"I should have known," was all Gary said when he saw her.

## Chapter 21

"**S**ounds like you two have had an exciting evening," Gary said after he took Joshua's statement. Maggie was sitting on her stool, with Poe stretched out on the counter and enjoying her undivided attention.

"You said a mouthful," Joshua replied as an EMT shined a penlight in his eyes.

"From what I can tell, you look all right, but you should probably go to the hospital just to be sure," said the guy wearing navy-blue pants and a matching windbreaker with EMT in bright-yellow letters splashed across the back.

"She almost fainted. You might want to check her out, too," Joshua said and pointed to Maggie.

Her eyes popped open wide. "I'm not going to the hospital. I didn't even hit my head. I don't like the sight of blood. That's all," she replied and frowned. Then she looked to the spot on the floor that Gary had already sectioned off with a little awkwardly placed yellow police tape.

"This little bit of blood?" Gary chuckled. "You should have seen the fellow who accidentally dropped a hatchet on his foot. Now that was a lot of..." Gary began, but the expression of disgust on not just Maggie's face but Joshua's too made him clear his throat instead.

"So," he continued, "you said the man tripped on his way out. Neither one of you have any cuts. I'm guessing that when he tripped, he stabbed himself. Judging by the blood, he may or may not show up at the hospital. Sometimes even a superficial wound can bleed a lot, but no stitches are required," Gary said as he wrote a few more notes.

"Do you think you'll catch him?" Joshua asked.

"Of course he'll catch him. This is Fair Haven. Not New York City. Plus, no one… is leaving town… with the weather," Maggie said as she glanced out the window.

A person was walking past, waving their arms and wailing. As soon as they saw the people in the bookstore, they flung the door open. Ruby Sinclair burst into the shop.

"My father will hear of this!" she shouted.

Maggie jumped off her stool and went to her side. Although Ruby was a weird one and certainly not on friendly terms with Maggie, she was near hysterics.

"Ruby, what happened?" she asked.

The woman reached behind her and clicked the door handle three times before answering. "My dress! It's ruined! My father will not stand for this type of behavior!" Ruby whimpered.

When Maggie looked down, a wave of light-headedness rushed over her. The front of Ruby's pastel dress was covered with blood. Keeping in mind that not just Joshua but Gary and the EMTs were still in the store, Maggie took a deep breath and focused on Ruby's tearful face.

"Have you been stabbed? Where are you hurt?" Maggie asked, taking Ruby's hands in hers and holding them more to keep herself steady than anything else. For good measure, Maggie also bit the inside of her mouth in order to keep herself aware and on her feet. The pinch of pain was enough to chase the light-headedness away.

"He grabbed me! He was no gentleman! My father will hear of this and have him arrested, and the key will be thrown in the river!" Ruby exclaimed, her arm flying up to drape dramatically over her eyes.

The EMTs rushed over to check her out, but they quickly discovered that she was not bleeding but had been bled on.

"Come with me, Ruby," Maggie said.

"Wait just a second." Gary stepped in. "I'll need to talk to her first."

"She's not going anywhere, Gary," Maggie replied. She slipped her arm through Ruby's as the strange woman turned over two books on the counter and then turned them back again.

"Look, I know you've been bitten by the mystery bug and think you are Detective Columbo, but this is serious. I need to talk to her and..." Gary stopped as Maggie squared her shoulders.

"This has nothing to do with that," Maggie said as she led Ruby to what had been Mr. Whitfield's cubby near the tiny kitchenette. She turned up the heat and sat Ruby down. The woman continued to babble, more to herself than to anyone else, as Maggie retrieved a small towel for her to dry her hands and face. She put a large mug of water in the microwave. Within a few seconds, the water was hot, and Maggie dropped a bag of mint tea into it before handing it to Ruby. Ruby, who was still frowning, her eyes brimming with tears, had been nervously arranging the pens in the cup on the desk by color.

"This is the most excitement Fair Haven has seen in a while," Gary said to Joshua.

"I should hope so. If it's going to be like this, I'm putting the 'for sale' sign in the window of this shop and heading back to Hartford," Joshua huffed.

"You aren't planning on leaving anytime soon," Gary said more than asked. "We still have a murder on our hands."

"You can't possibly still believe I had something to do with Bo's death," Joshua balked.

"I'm just saying that the case is still open. We don't have anyone in custody yet. But we've got our eye on a few people," Gary replied with a smile. "What was Maggie doing here after the store had closed?"

"You know, I have no idea. She didn't tell me." Joshua got up and walked over to the kitchenette. Gary was close behind him.

"Mr. Whitfield always said that mint tea calmed the nerves. I don't know if that's really true, but we'll try it." She soothed Ruby, who had moved on from pencils to undoing the ball of rubber bands that had been on the desk for years. "I miss him. He was sort of like my father," Maggie said.

The words caught Ruby's attention for a second, and she looked up from her task. For the first time in a long time, a smile came across Ruby's face. But she quickly continued fussing with the ball of rubber bands.

Maggie handed her the cup of tea, which she took daintily. The women sat there for a few minutes like old friends as Ruby sipped from her steaming mug before Gary cleared his throat.

"Ruby, are you all right to talk to me for a few moments?" Gary asked politely.

Ruby lifted her chin, looked down her nose, and gave a quick nod. Maggie stood up, set her mug in the tiny sink, and left the two alone. She walked past Joshua to get her umbrella and was about to leave the shop when Joshua stopped her.

"Where are you going?"

"Home," she said and looked around as if Joshua had just asked her the craziest question in the history of conversation.

"You can't go home. We had a break-in. Someone stole our merchandise," Joshua said.

"I told you who it was," Maggie replied with another eye roll.

"You never said what you were doing here," Joshua said.

Maggie felt as if she'd been caught stealing money from the till. She'd come here to tell Joshua what Roger Hawes had said to her, that the grumpy old frump had come to her house to tell her Joshua was a cheat and was getting a big insurance check. She swallowed hard and looked up at him. Darn him! After the night they'd had, he looked as if he'd just stepped off the page of some rugged hunting or carpentry magazine. She didn't dare stare into his eyes, or she'd fall into them.

"Do you think I had something to do with this?" Maggie felt as if her eyes were going to pop out of her head.

"No. I guess not," Joshua replied then scratched his head. "I don't know what I'm thinking. I'm a mess."

"I came to tell you that Roger Hawes was at my house," she muttered.

"What did he want?"

"He wanted to tell me that…you were getting a big payout from the insurance company for Bo's death." She swallowed hard. "That you wouldn't care what happened to anyone if they got hurt here."

"What?" Joshua's shoulders slumped, and when Maggie did peer up at him, he looked as if he'd been slapped across the face. "What is it with the people in this town? My father was here for decades, and there wasn't a single person to speak poorly of him."

Maggie thought of Toby Hodgkin but didn't think telling Joshua about that lying snake would be of much comfort.

"I'm here two weeks, and I've been tried and convicted in the court of public opinion, and I haven't even done anything." He shook his head.

"I don't think that's true. You had a lot of people show up here tonight. They came to see your new café. They weren't scared of you," Maggie said.

"Why do I suddenly get the feeling they all came to see the man who killed Bo Logan before the police drag me off in handcuffs?" Joshua looked down at his feet. "And for the record, I don't get a big payout because a man died on the job. I get a big premium increase, which I also can't afford on top of everything else."

"I never thought you killed Bo. And I know Roger. He's got a reputation a mile long for being a cheapskate. Sort of the pot calling the kettle black. He talks tough, but really, he's not," Maggie replied. She could tell what Joshua was about to say before he said it and shook her head. "But I don't think he's capable of murder, either."

Gary stepped out from the back of the shop and quickly tucked his notebook into his pocket before letting out a long sigh.

"Did you get anything from her?" Joshua asked.

"Yeah, she was grabbed by a shadow that had finished mopping the floor, and it bled all over her," Gary replied. "She's arranging your paperclips by size. I'm sure that will be a great help to you."

"Thanks, Gary," Maggie said softly before a giant yawn stretched her mouth wide.

"Yeah, thanks, Gary," Joshua said with a little more attitude.

"I don't think there is anything else we can do from this point," Gary said as he waved to the EMTs that they could go. But just as he was about to say goodbye to Joshua and Maggie, his radio burst to life.

"*Gary, you still out there at the bookstore?*" It was Lola, the dispatcher.

"Yes, Lola. Now what?"

"*We got a serious emergency at the Hickory Creek Bridge. Someone tried to get across. We need everyone out there. He's in bad shape,*" she said in a staticky voice.

"Copy that. I'm on my way. EMTs still on the premises. I'll have them tag along. Ten-four. Over and out."

"Who would try to drive through that? Everyone knows it's flooded," Maggie said.

"I didn't know it was flooded," Joshua replied and shrugged.

"Right. You aren't from here. Okay, I'm going home. Tired. What a night," Maggie said and quickly grabbed her umbrella. "Make sure Ruby gets on her way safely. Night!"

Before either of the men knew what she was up to, Maggie was in her car and heading to the Hickory Creek Bridge. Everyone in town knew it was flooded.

## Chapter 22

"You're off your rocker, Margaret. That's all I can say. Ever since Mr. Whitfield died and his son showed up in town, it's as if everything has been turned upside down, including yourself," Maggie said as she sped as fast as the slick roads would allow to the Hickory Creek Bridge.

The rain wasn't as bad as it had been. The windshield wipers kept up with the droplets, and she could see even in the dark. But it was relentless and showed no sign of it slowing up. The puddles on the side of the road made swooshing sounds and pulled at the wheels of her car, dragging them slightly as she drove through. Huge waves of dirty water washed up onto the sidewalks.

But the closer Maggie got to Hickory Creek Bridge, the darker it became. The shops that stood shoulder to shoulder in downtown Fair Haven began to spread out and give each other breathing room. The businesses became less trendy and more practical as she drove down the road. Insurance offices, law offices, Mac's Garage, one of Roger Hawes's pawnshops, a currency exchange, and a closed Long John Silver's fast food restaurant peppered the landscape, becoming fewer and farther between. It didn't take long for large trees to be the

146

only things on either side of the road. The ditches on either side became steeper and steeper as she approached the bridge.

"Why are you out here?" she wondered out loud to herself. "The police aren't even here yet. The fire department. No one is here yet, and maybe it's not him. Maybe some yahoo from town got drunk and made a wrong turn toward the bridge instead of heading directly home." It was possible.

But something in Maggie's gut told her that the person who had crashed was Heath Toonsley. She just knew it was. He'd have no idea that the bridge would be impossible to cross if he had been away at Harvard for years. Besides, the Toonsleys were fairly new to Fair Haven. Even if Samantha and Calvin knew better than to try to cross the bridge after so many rainy days, that didn't mean Heath had ever paid enough attention to the locals talking to learn anything.

Before she could get close to the bridge itself, the water had started to puddle in a lot more places. Up ahead, shining brightly in her headlights, were the reflectors of the construction barrels blocking the road—or at least partially blocking it. The Bridge Closed signs were off to the side of the road. From what Maggie could see, it looked as if a car had quickly driven through the barricade of barrels, pushing them apart. Maggie was not going to take any chances on losing her car or on getting in the way of the emergency vehicles that had to be getting closer by now.

Without hesitating, she put her car in reverse and backed up to where there was no indication that the pavement would be underwater anytime soon. She parked and grabbed her umbrella and a flashlight from her glove compartment. Besides a flashlight, she had flares, matches, and three glow sticks. In her trunk, she had jumper cables, two blankets, a shovel, and some cat litter, which was cheaper and easier to haul around than the heavy bags of salt for any time she might get stuck in the snow. But at the moment, she just wanted the flashlight.

As soon as she opened the door, she could hear the sound of a fire truck blasting its horn off in the distance.

"You're insane, Maggie. Mr. Whitfield's death affected you more than you know. All this because some jerk absconded with one of his precious tomes. *Sierra Madre Heights* has to be ruined by now," she mumbled to herself as she hurried between the two barrels in the direction of the bridge.

The water wasn't high at this point. The pavement was wet, and there were a handful of puddles that didn't appear to be getting any larger. Still, Maggie knew this was deceptive. As she came over the top of the hill, all she could barely see by the light of her flashlight was the ghostly railing peeking up above the water that was rushing over the bridge. And then, like the eyes of some hellish monster, yellow hazard lights from a car blinked from beneath the water.

"If you can't see the ground, go around. Doesn't everyone learn that in driver's education?" Maggie muttered to herself as she shined the light on the car.

Sitting on the edge of the open driver's-side window was a frantically waving man. He wore a black hat and an expensive-looking raincoat over a black shirt. From where she was, Maggie couldn't see his face through the rain. She inched closer to try to get a better look.

"Are you all right?" she shouted.

"No! I'm hurt!" he called back and pointed to his side.

"The police are on the way!" Maggie said. She wrinkled her nose as a fine mist swept beneath her umbrella. The sound of the sirens was definitely getting closer.

"Help me!" the man shouted. "The water has filled the car!"

"Just wait!" Maggie shouted.

"Help me! I'm going to die!" he screamed.

The rain was starting to come down harder. Maggie didn't know if it was her imagination, but it sounded as if the water was starting to rush even faster. Lightning flashed, and a crack of thunder rolled over the sky with such force Maggie could feel it in her chest.

"I'm going to die! I can't swim!" the man screamed.

"Just wait!" Maggie tried to shout over the rain and water.

But she was sure the guy didn't hear a word of what she was saying. He was pounding the roof of the car. From what Maggie could see, his eyes were wild with fear.

Quickly, she looked around, hoping she might see something that would at least give the man some comfort to hang on to. But before she could spot anything, a wave of water swept quickly up to the car, slamming it into the guardrail. There were several tall trees not far from the car, but the man would have to try to balance on the hood of his car and jump just a foot or two.

"Right, Mags. Jump just a foot or two…in the rain…at night. Good plan. Real good," she said to herself.

Still, it was all she had. If she could convince the man to just sit tight a few more minutes, maybe he could stay where he was. If the only option was to jump and risk falling into the cold water, she'd hang on to the car.

She shouted for the man to hold on, but just as she was about to go back to her car, a flash of lightning struck a nearby tree. Sparks flew everywhere. Maggie gasped and blinked to get her eyes to focus again just as she saw the glowing red embers start to tip. The sound of branches snapping and the groan of the tree trunk breaking in half were almost as loud as the tree trunk hitting the car.

Maggie took a few steps forward. The water rushed around her ankles. She couldn't do anything. If she went even a little farther, the current would surely sweep her into the icy darkness. The eerie glow of the hazard lights still flashed. Where were the ambulance and fire truck? How could she have gotten there so much sooner than them?

But just as she was about to really start to panic, she saw a hand stretch over the trunk of the tree that was lying on top of the car. The man had somehow lost his cap. Maggie focused on him and was sure that it was Heath Toonsley. His face was white, and his eyes and nose were red from crying and the cold.

A strange mixture of emotions swirled inside Maggie as she watched him holding on to the fallen tree, which had completely caved in the back window and trunk of his car. He'd snuck into the bookshop and knocked Joshua unconscious so he could get his hands on a book worth some money. His family had money, so what had this been for? The thrill of it? Just to say he'd done it? Maggie was certain it wasn't because he wanted to read the first edition of *Sierra Madre Heights*.

She shook her head. It wasn't that she wanted the man to drown. Of course she didn't. But she didn't mind seeing him scared and shivering in the cold. After he'd pulled a knife on her and scared poor Ruby Sinclair into hysterics, it was a fitting end to his adventure. And although she'd never admit it and have people think she was horrible, she couldn't help but feel the most regret for the book that was now soaked beyond all repair and probably half washed down Hickory Creek by now.

As luck would have it, if Maggie was to call it luck, the tree that had fallen gave Heath a bridge to another tree and another—if he was brave enough to climb on them. Maggie squinted and shined her flashlight along the fallen tree. Sure enough, if Heath would climb out of the car and crawl along the trunk to the next tree, which looked thick and sturdy, he could grab hold of one of the low branches and pull himself up. She swung her light back to him. He was scowling with frustration.

"Crawl on the trunk to that tree!" she shouted. "Then climb onto the next tree and the next!" She tried to point and shout instructions, but Heath wouldn't move. She'd have to go get him. Maggie was angry. How could a young man like him not understand that he just needed to climb the trees and he'd be safe?

"Fine! Idiot!" she shouted but was sure he didn't hear her.

Maggie folded her umbrella and set it on the ground near the base of the nearest tree. She climbed up into the branches easily; everyone in Fair Haven knew how to climb trees if they'd had any kind of childhood here. Even in the rain, she could easily maneuver herself from branch to branch, and before she knew it, she had crossed over to the next tree, getting closer to Heath. She shined her light at him, and he waved back.

"I'm not saying hello, Heath! Get up on the tree trunk!" she shouted.

But he shook his head. Did he really expect her to hold his hand all the way from his sinking car to safety?

Maggie inched closer. By this time, she was soaked through. But when she was about to get to the fallen tree, something inside told her to freeze. She shined her light in Heath's direction. He was not only on the fallen tree, but he was scrambling to get to her. He wasn't as hurt or scared as he pretended. He wanted to hurt her.

"You ruined everything!" he screamed.

"I'm trying to help you!" Maggie replied.

"You'll help me by drowning in this river!" he shouted back.

Maggie quickly reversed her movements. She was not afraid of climbing the tree even in the rain. But as Heath tried to get his footing on the tree that had fallen on his car, he slipped. Now he was in real trouble, because his grip wasn't strong, and he wouldn't be able to hang on with the cold water continually pushing past him.

Maggie went back the way she'd come, muttering some very unladylike names for Heath Toonsley. Back on solid ground, she picked up her umbrella, opened it, and watched as Heath struggled. Why would he do that? What was wrong with him?

The fire truck was the first to arrive. The giant monster of a vehicle screeched to a halt about twenty feet from Maggie, where the water was starting to creep higher. A police car joined it, and a familiar form stepped out of it and hurried up to her.

"Maggie, what are you doing here?" Gary barked through the sound of rain and the wind, which was starting to pick up.

"It's him. It's Heath Toonsley. But I'll bet the book is hardly recognizable by now," Maggie replied.

"Come on. Let's get you out of here." Gary took Maggie's umbrella and held it over both of them as he put his arm around her shoulder and led her back to her own car.

The firemen had immediately assessed the situation. They pulled a steel cable with a giant hook at the end of it from a winch at the front of the huge red truck. One brave man in a fluorescent jacket waded into the cold water. Only then did Maggie realize how strong the current over the bridge really was. More than once, the fireman lost his footing and was swept farther away from Heath Toonsley, only to struggle and strain to get back on course and make his way toward the drowned car, the fallen tree, and Heath.

Maggie didn't say anything until she got into her car. "Will you be taking him to the police station?"

"Yeah, eventually. He'll have to go to the hospital first. He's probably frozen and waterlogged," Gary huffed. "Why?"

"He just stole from Mr. Whitfield. I'd like to know why," Maggie said.

"Look, Maggie. Go home. It's going to rain all night, and this is going to take a while," Gary soothed.

"But don't you understand? He stole that book, and now it's ruined. It's not something that you can just look up and order. It was one of a kind." Maggie sighed.

"Well, it takes one to know one, Mags," Gary said. "I'll

make you a deal. If you go right home and get some rest, I'll call you when he's at the police station. I won't be able to question him until then anyway. The doctors will be poking and prodding him all night."

"Promise, Gary?"

"I promise if you promise to go home and get some rest. Don't make me send out a squad car to make sure you are snug in your bed," Gary replied.

Maggie made it home quickly and was happy to get out of her wet clothes. She was sure that she wasn't going to get any sleep while waiting for Gary's phone call. But as soon as her head hit the pillow, she was out. Not until she dreamed about a phone ringing did she snap her eyes open and realize the sun was coming up.

"Hello?" she muttered.

"He's on his way to the station. I hope you don't mind, but I called Joshua too," Gary said with a slight hesitation in his voice.

"Why would I mind? It was his store that was robbed. Even if he doesn't care about the books, it still is his place," Maggie grumbled.

"Atta girl. See you when you get here," Gary replied.

Almost before he'd even hung up the phone, she was out of bed, dressed, and nearly out the door.

## Chapter 23

The Fair Haven police station was a small white building with black shutters. The front door was glass and opened with a pull. Black bars across all the windows might have made the place look scary save for the flower boxes that hung from each one. They were tended by Felix Porter, the florist, who had his shop just two doors down. The perfectly manicured shrubs and cobblestone walkway gave the place a real homey feel. Even on this drizzly morning, as Maggie pulled up, she thought the place looked warm and inviting. Of course, she wasn't the one being booked there. She was the one going to press charges against that person. For all she knew, Heath Toonsley thought the little white building looked like the entrance to Hades.

"Abandon all hope, ye who enter here...except me," Maggie muttered to herself as the memory of her ordeal with Heath came to mind. "I hope they throw the book at him. No pun intended."

She trotted to the front door and gave it a yank. Inside, the soothing smell of cinnamon and apples hit her nose.

"Maggie Bell?" the receptionist, Gloria Teeble, chirped. "Why, I haven't seen you for some time. I guess that's good, since I work at the police station. If I'd seen you often, I'd say there was something wrong with you." A Yankee Candle Company candle burned happily on the counter, the source of the soothing smell.

"Hi, Gloria. Yes," Maggie replied before pushing her glasses up on her nose and looking down at the floor.

Even though Fair Haven was a small town where everyone knew everyone, Maggie never felt comfortable chatting. She never knew what to say, and now was no different. Even though she had plenty to spill regarding her opinion of what had happened the previous night, Maggie couldn't find a single word to share with Gloria.

"Officer Brookes is waiting for you in his conference room," Gloria said. She smiled as she stood up to unlatch the small swinging half door that separated the waiting area from the police area.

A couple of desks behind Gloria held more family photos than paperwork or files. Had the words "Police Department" not been stenciled in big black letters over the front door, this office could have easily passed for a calm insurance or real estate office. And if no one looked into the far back corner, where there was a small cubby with an iron gated door, no one would ever suspect that criminals were held there.

Gloria had to be in her sixties, with salt-and-pepper hair and a full figure, and could have been a receptionist or even a bank teller. But the sidearm she wore was threatening enough to intimidate Dirty Harry and was another little detail that reminded a person they were not in a simple office. They were in the pokey.

Maggie thanked Gloria and quickly walked through the office to the conference room. The door was closed. She took a deep breath and knocked softly.

"C'mon in!" Gary barked. Maggie carefully turned the knob and stuck her head in first before entering.

"So where is he?" Maggie asked.

"He's on his way. You know how long it takes for hospitals to release someone," Gary replied as he pulled a chair out for her next to him at the long table. There were posters of McGruff the Crime Dog on the wall, as well as a large rectangular bulletin board with OSHA rules and the Heimlich maneuver tacked up on it.

"It was Heath Toonsley, right?" Maggie asked as she took a seat.

"It was. He was very grateful to the Fair Haven Fire Department for pulling him from the submerged Mercedes that was pinned beneath that tree. Not that it was going anywhere but farther down the creek." Gary chuckled.

"What about the book?" Maggie asked.

"How did I know you were going to ask about that?" Gary replied.

He stood up and walked over to a small table, where he grabbed a large plastic bag. Inside were the swollen, warped remains of the first edition of *Sierra Madre Heights*.

"Put it away. I don't want to see it." Maggie frowned.

Gary did as she asked then sat down to take an official statement from her regarding the events that had taken place the previous evening. When Maggie revealed why she had been at the shop after the party, Gary had to shake his head.

"That Roger Hawes is a blowhard if ever there was one. Someday, he's going to tattle on the wrong person, and they are going to really put him in his place," Gary replied as he wrote the notes on a long yellow pad.

"Gary, did you really think Joshua had killed Bo?" Maggie asked.

Gary looked up at her from beneath his dark-brown eyelashes. "No. But I'm still not sure what happened. I'm hoping our little friend will be able to clear some things up. He was so traumatized last night that he spilled quite a bit of information."

"Like what?" Maggie leaned forward.

"Like he never meant to kill anyone." Gary scoffed. "Not exactly a confession, but pretty close to one if you ask me."

Before Maggie could ask any more questions, they heard shouting and cursing coming from the lobby.

"Stay behind me," Gary said as he hurried and opened the conference room door. There in the waiting area of the police station was a frazzled and wild-looking Heath Toonsley shouting at Gloria and a uniformed officer Maggie had seen around town. She was pretty sure his name was Tim.

"Settle down!" Tim shouted.

"Get these things off me! Do you know who I am? Do you know who my parents are? I'll have your job for this. And yours, too!" Heath shouted at Gloria, who yawned.

"You need to get in the pen before I take those off of you," Officer Tim replied as he slipped his hand around Heath's biceps.

"The pen? A pen is for animals! I want my parents here immediately!" Heath shouted as Tim tugged him in the direction of the small cell in the corner of the office.

"Yeah, yeah. Mommy and Daddy will be here soon enough. You've got time," Tim said. As he urged Heath in the direction of the pen, Heath wasted no time knocking papers and the photos off each desk he passed.

"Now, was that really necessary, young man?" Gloria shouted. "Your mama might put up with your shenanigans, but around here, you show respect for other people's property. Tim?"

Tim turned Heath around, grabbed him by the scruff of the neck, and squeezed. "Tell Gloria we're sorry and that it was an accident."

"What? I will not!" Heath shouted.

Tim, who looked as harmless as a school crossing guard, took hold of Heath's ear and gave it a twist. He yowled like a cat that had gotten its tail caught beneath a rocking chair.

"Sorry! Sorry!" Heath shrieked before Tim let go of his ear and pulled him toward the small jail cell.

Without any more resistance, he was able to get Heath inside the tiny cubicle and slam the door shut with a clang. "Put your wrists through the slat," Tim ordered.

Heath did as he was told but not without muttering more to himself than for Tim to hear. With the handcuffs removed, Heath rubbed his wrists and scowled at Tim.

"Heath, I'm surprised that you are being so ungrateful to the officer who helped get you out of the water yesterday. Most college students can read a warning sign indicating a bridge is out. You must have been out that day," Gary teased as Maggie watched from safely behind him.

Before Heath could say anything else, Joshua came through the front door. Gloria greeted him with the same cheery disposition she had Maggie, as if Heath's disruption had been nothing more than a mosquito to be swatted away and forgotten.

"Joshua, I'm glad you could make it down," Gary said with his hand extended.

As Maggie looked at Joshua, she suddenly realized that he and Heath had very similar features. The same height. Same light hair color. If Heath had been wearing a bulky jacket, like he had been yesterday, when Bo Logan had been killed, it would have been easy for someone to confuse him with Joshua fleeing the bookstore. But Maggie wondered who that witness had been who Gary said had claimed spotted Joshua making tracks from the scene.

"Officer Brookes," Joshua replied coldly but accepted his hand to shake.

"Maggie, if you'll excuse us a moment, I need to talk to Joshua in private," Gary said.

Maggie nodded and tried to slip past both men without any further conversation. But Joshua had a different idea.

"How are you doing?" he asked.

"Fine. Fine." Maggie gave a flash of a smile as she looked at Joshua then quickly at her feet.

"I'm not sure why you have to be here, but this should be quick," Joshua said.

"Oh, maybe it's because Junior over there had a knife on me last night. That might be why. I'm just guessing though," she said almost apologetically.

"Right." Joshua nodded. "I had blocked that out. It was too much to think of."

"Of course." Maggie hurried toward Gloria to have a seat in the waiting area at the front of the station.

Gloria, trained to observe, smirked as she watched Maggie slip past Gary and Joshua. Maggie took a seat, her knees pressed tightly together, and folded her hands in her lap only after she pushed her glasses up.

"You know, that isn't uncommon," Gloria replied.

"What's not?" Maggie asked.

"That people block out certain aspects of a crime committed against them," Gloria replied. "Especially if it is something really scary."

"How come I remember it?" Maggie asked, not intending to be short with Gloria but unable to do anything about her tone now.

"Because it happened to you. Mr. Whitfield was probably more scared for you than he was for himself. The mind sometimes needs a while to dissect everything that's happened and then come up with a way to cope. It doesn't mean he doesn't care," Gloria said before taking a seat behind her desk.

"I don't care if he cares. I just work for him," Maggie chirped before focusing on her nails as if there was something too interesting to ignore.

"I was in that old bookstore a couple of times. I really liked Mr. Whitfield. He was a charming man. Very educated," Gloria said.

Maggie looked up. "He was very smart."

"I remember he had a cat. A pretty black creature with green eyes."

"That's Poe. He's still there."

As Gloria chatted with Maggie, a ruckus came from the pen. Heath was pacing back and forth, mumbling and coughing like a little boy trying to get attention.

"I'll have to stop in there again sometime," Gloria continued.

"Joshua has changed the place a bit. There are more books, and there is a café, and he's talking about putting in a lounge, too." Maggie found it easy to talk to Gloria after knowing that she'd been in the bookshop. But as she tried to talk, in the background, Heath just got louder and louder.

"I'm entitled to a phone call! I want to know where my parents are!" he whined.

"I hate when they get loud," Gloria remarked. "If there was anyone else in that cell with him, he wouldn't be saying a peep. Funny how pretty boys like him seem to clam up when a real career criminal is sharing their space."

Just then, tires screeched on the slick pavement outside. Bright headlights nearly blinded Maggie as she looked out the glass door and saw a silver Lexus SUV come to a stop in front of the police station. The very angry-looking Calvin and Samantha Toonsley appeared, she with an umbrella to protect her hair from the rain and he with a Titleist baseball hat on.

Mr. Toonsley yanked the door open and stomped inside. "Where is my son?" he barked.

"Dad!" Heath shouted.

"Mr. Toonsley, you son is under arrest for robbery, assault with a deadly weapon, and the murder of Bo Logan," Gloria said calmly.

"What?" Samantha almost screamed before she focused on Gloria. "Where is he? I want to see him immediately!"

"He's in the pen, ma'am. You'll get to speak to him soon enough," Gloria replied.

Meanwhile, Maggie watched as Samantha flipped her hair, shifted from one foot to the other, and tried to sweet-talk Gloria into letting her visit her son. Nothing worked. She was amazed at how cool Gloria remained even as Samantha and Calvin switched tactics and ganged up on her.

"I'll have my lawyer here, and you'll be sorry. Son! Don't say a word!" Calvin turned back to Gloria. "You'll be sorry for this. You're going to be out of a job."

Gary and Joshua emerged from the conference room. "Your son already confessed," Gary said.

"That's not true, Dad. He's lying!" Maggie heard Heath say.

With Gary there and Tim not far away, Gloria opened the half door and let everyone come in. As soon as Samantha saw her son peeking out of the cell, his hands wrapped helplessly around the bars, she ran to him.

"Is there any real reason he's locked up like this?" Samantha demanded and pointed at Joshua. "This is an outrage. You obviously have the wrong person. The right person is standing right there."

"Gary, I want to know what in the heck you have my boy locked up like a darn animal in a cage for. My lawyers are on their way and..." Calvin started. He was a lot calmer than Samantha, and as Maggie studied his face, she was sure she saw a hint of concern that what he was about to hear was indeed his boy's fault.

"Samantha, calm down," Gary ordered.

"Not while he's chained up in there. This is cruel and unusual punishment! I'll have your jobs," she hollered, sounding just as spoiled and rude as her son had just a few minutes ago.

"Heath confessed, last night, after we rescued him from the Hickory Creek Bridge, to flipping the electrical switch at the Bookish Café bookshop and intentionally electrocuting Bo," Gary said.

"It's a lie, Mom. They threatened me! They made me say it," Heath blubbered.

"What? That's crazy," Samantha said. "Why would he do that?"

"To get the book and sell it for the money," Maggie muttered. Everyone stopped and looked at her.

"You can just mind your business, Little Miss Bookworm," Samantha snapped. "Heath doesn't need money. We have plenty of money. More than everyone in this room combined."

Before Samantha could even finish the sentence, Calvin pulled out a chair and sat down. He looked at his son, and his face turned stoic.

"I'm sorry, Samantha, but we have a witness who can place Heath fleeing from the scene. He almost got away with it. It was looking very much like Josh was our main suspect. But criminals are criminals because they aren't that bright," Gary said. "He didn't get what he was looking for the first time. He had to go back. Stealing a book worth ten thousand dollars? How hard could that be, right, Heath?"

"Ten thousand…that's nothing. If he needed money, he would have come to us," Samantha said. But when she looked at her husband, it was her turn to grow pale. "Cal, what is it? What's wrong with you? Why are you just sitting there, letting them crucify your son?"

"You did it, didn't you," Calvin barely whispered.

"It's your fault!" Heath shouted at his father. "I wouldn't have had to do it if you didn't cut me off! Dad cut me off and told me if I said anything to you, I'd be out of the will for good," Heath shouted before looking to his mother. "And you! I wouldn't be in this mess if you'd just bought the book!"

"What?" Samantha looked hurt and confused at her son's accusation.

"If you had just bought the book like you'd been bragging

to everyone you were going to do, I wouldn't have had to try to get it myself!" Heath shouted.

His face was red with anger of all things. Maggie realized there was not a shred of remorse for not just what he'd done to Bo but for how he was talking to his parents right now. His eyes blazed, and had he not been behind those bars, who knew what he would have done to them.

"If I bought it, it would have been mine. Were you going to steal it from me?" Samantha asked.

Heath said nothing but just scowled at his mother.

Maggie also couldn't tell if Samantha was more upset that her son had killed a man and tried to hurt Joshua and herself or that he was willing to steal from her.

"What happened to your shirt?" Samantha pointed to the rip in his black shirt.

Beneath it, Maggie saw a quick flash of white bandage.

"Well, when your son decided to pull a knife on Miss Bell," Gary said, "he accidentally tripped and stabbed himself. Then he bled all over the floor in the bookshop and poor Ruby Sinclair, as if she doesn't have enough problems of her own. She can testify to his fleeing the bookshop in a hurry and carrying the stolen book with him. There's also a little detail called DNA that puts him there. So he's looking at murder, attempted murder, and theft."

"Don't say another word, do you hear me?" Calvin stood up and approached the bars. Now it was Heath's turn to look afraid. "Don't you say a darn thing until the lawyers get here. Then we'll go home and figure out what to do…"

Just then, Sheriff Lee Smith came waltzing into the office. He had been in several Strong Man competitions in the late nineties and early two thousands. Although at first glance, someone might think he had had his fair share of donuts, all he had to do was remove his coat, as he did now, and they'd see the short sleeves of his shirt struggling around his bulging biceps. His pants suffered in a similar fashion over his thigh muscles.

"Oh, no. He's not going home. Morning, Gloria. Coffee ready?" Lee asked.

"It's in your office," Gloria replied without looking up from her paperwork.

"My goodness, it's like a regular town hall meeting in here. Gary, what are all these people doing here?" the sheriff asked. He strutted past the desks, Maggie, Joshua, and the Toonsleys, who were standing next to the cell from which Heath peeked out.

Gary cleared his throat and made all the proper introductions before the sheriff nodded. "All right then, get their statements and see if this young man would like to have a discussion in private with you once you are done," Sheriff Lee said then turned to go to his office.

"Sheriff, we'd like to take our son home now. If you could let him out of this cage, we'll discuss what's to be done with our lawyer and be back tomorrow. By the way, I think I remember seeing you at the golf club a few weeks back. Didn't know you were a member, but now that I do, we'll have to hit a few balls together," Calvin said with a smile.

"I'm sorry, Mr. Toonsley, but that isn't how things work. Your son will remain in our custody. A court date will be set, and then bail will be arranged. Until then, he's staying put," the sheriff said before slipping into his office and shutting the door.

"Mom, you can't leave me here. Dad, this is what they do to people without any money. I don't belong here! Do something! Get me out of here! I won't stay here! This is not fair!" Heath was nearly hopping up and down in a tantrum to rival a hungry toddler who had missed his nap.

"Calm down. You're making a scene that these people will spread all over town," Samantha scolded as she tried to calm her son.

"I don't care! Get me out of here!" Heath screamed.

Joshua walked over to Maggie, and his eyes were wide with shock at the display taking place. "I need to talk to you."

"About what?" Maggie replied and pushed her glasses up on her nose.

"Not here," Joshua said.

Maggie's heart began to pound. She wasn't sure if she was ready for any more conversations or meetings with Joshua. After everything that had happened, she felt as if she hadn't slept at all.

"Where is my car? I'll at least drive it home," Calvin barked at Gary.

"Your Mercedes is at the impound. I don't believe she'll run anymore. She was underwater for over half an hour," Tim replied. "The hazard lights had been on when we arrived, but by the time we were able to pull Heath from the car, it was good night, Irene. Plus, the tree that fell on it didn't do you any favors."

Calvin bit his lip and looked at Samantha, who was still standing by Heath, unwilling to believe that he'd really done anything wrong.

"You two are free to go. I'll call you if I have any more questions," Gary said to Maggie and Joshua before turning his attention to the Toonsley family.

Maggie wrapped her arms around herself and hustled to the door. She fumbled awkwardly with the little latch that kept the half door from swinging open.

"I'll get that for you," Gloria said. "I'll stop by the book-shop soon."

"That would be great," Maggie replied. She stepped back out into the drizzle, which had decided to remain just a fine mist.

"Wait, where are you rushing to? Have you got a date?" Joshua joked as he followed Maggie outside.

"No. I don't," she huffed.

"Well, I know today is your usual day off, but I was hoping that you could stop by the café?" Joshua asked.

"I'm afraid I can't. I've got a million errands to run, and I won't have any time during the week to get to them," she said. She got to her car and yanked the driver's-side door open before collapsing her umbrella and tossing it into the passenger seat.

"I guess it can wait until tomorrow." Joshua shrugged.

"Good. Okay. I'll see you tomorrow," Maggie huffed before getting in her car and pulling away. She watched Joshua for a second in the rearview mirror but then quickly focused on the road.

"He wanted to talk to you alone in the bookshop. You said no. Too busy," she scolded herself. "What errands were those that you were babbling about, Margaret? You don't have any errands. You don't have anything to do." She twisted her mouth to the right. "Could you be a bigger dope? Probably not. But it's still early."

## Chapter 24

As Maggie left her house the following morning, she had to admit she'd barely slept a wink. Whatever Joshua Whitfield wanted to speak to her about had tickled at the back of her mind every time she sat down to do something. While she had been doing her laundry, writing her schedule for the week, or trying to read her book, his handsome face had kept creeping into view. She had gone to sleep convincing herself he was probably going to cut her hours or let her go altogether in order to hire someone with pink hair or those loopy things in their ears to give the bookshop a more contemporary edge.

"You're imagining things," she muttered as she drove her familiar route to work. The leaves were slowly starting to change as the colder weather was getting ready to settle in.

Her gut folded over on itself as she drove to the shop. There was a parking spot right in front, and when she got out of the car, she thought the day had started strangely, the same way it had the day Mr. Whitfield had died. The memory of that didn't make her feel any better. She walked to the door and was about to unlock it but discovered it was already open. Joshua was already up and about and waiting for her.

When she walked in, the pleasant smell of coffee was wafting through the place. Maggie set her umbrella behind the counter and rubbed her sweating hands on her skirt.

"Margaret? Is that you?" Joshua yelled from the café side.

Maggie took a deep breath, squared her shoulders, and leaned through the door that joined the shops. "Yes," she said without emotion.

"Good," was all Joshua said. He looked adorable in a white apron over his T-shirt and blue jeans as he stood behind the new counter and finished installing some contraption that probably made a coffee drink no one had ever heard of.

"What is it you wanted to talk to me about?" Maggie folded her arms over her chest.

"Let's go into the bookstore. I think you might want to have a seat," Joshua replied.

"Look, if you are going to fire me, just do it. I'm not a child. I can handle rejection. And although I know more about how the bookstore operates than you do, I understand that we just don't click." Maggie had prepared this speech but hadn't expected to just launch into it.

"Fire you?"

Maggie pinched her lips together and pushed her glasses up on her nose.

"Why would I fire you? Everyone in town knows you work here. I'm not going to fire you. Do you ever think a pleasant thought, or is it all doom and gloom all day, every day?" Joshua put his hands on his hips and chuckled at her.

"You know what they say: hope for the best but prepare for the worst," Maggie replied. "What do you mean, everyone in town knows me? I don't know anyone in town. I've seen them, yes. I might recognize them in a lineup of sorts. But I don't really know anyone. And I like it that way."

"You are too much," Joshua said and walked to the bookshop.

Maggie followed him to what had been his father's cubby.

There was a stack of books with a red ribbon around them. One of the books was the first edition of *Sierra Madre Heights* that she'd thought Heath Toonsley had stolen and then ruined in his flooded car.

"What is all this?" Maggie asked.

"My dad had a will. He knew I'd want to try to make the business work. So he left me the building and his apartment and all of his treasures up there." Joshua smiled. "But he left you these books."

"What?" Maggie was so shocked she forgot about being awkward around Joshua.

"Yeah, that's why I couldn't let Heath Toonsley or his mother have *Sierra Madre Heights*. Had the guy had half a brain cell working, he might have noticed I gave him a copy of the 1969 second edition of *Webster's Dictionary*."

"I don't believe it," Maggie breathed as she regarded the books in the pretty red bow. "How did you find them? I mean, there was a rather elaborate system set up here and…"

"When I saw you hadn't thrown out any books, I just peeked around. I found your hiding spot behind the books already shelved about a week ago. After I reviewed Dad's will, I slowly collected the books and put them all together. I was going to give them to you sooner, but with all the excitement around, I had to wait." Joshua smiled.

"But they belong to you," Maggie said.

"No. Like I said, Dad left me the business. Now it's up to me to get it going. He left these for you. I don't really read."

Maggie glared at Joshua as if he'd just admitted to eating raw liver.

"In his will, he said he never paid you very well. These are worth some money. His instructions were that you were to sell them if the need arose to buy yourself a small house and live a happy life."

Maggie felt her eyes sting with tears as she touched the red ribbon. All this time, she'd been worrying about her future, and that rascal Mr. Whitfield had, from the grave, in one fell swoop, given her a solid foundation to build on. He'd had some secrets, that cunning old man. All this time, Maggie had thought he was just a pleasant fellow who loved books like she did, when in fact he had been helping people all over town without her even knowing. And now he had helped her in a way she'd never have expected.

"Who put this on there?" she asked quietly, gently touching the ribbon.

"I did," Joshua admitted. "I wanted it to look like a gift."

There was no stopping a couple tears from rolling down her cheeks. Maggie swallowed hard and picked up the books. They smelled old and musty like a good book should. In addition to *Sierra Madre Heights*, there was a first edition of *Gone With the Wind*, *King Philip's Chair*, *Ivanhoe*, *The Whip*, *The Hoosier Schoolmaster*, and *Fallen Timber*.

"Your father was a wonderful man," Maggie replied.

"Well, he obviously thought very highly of you too."

"I've got just the place for them in my house," Maggie gushed.

"Great. And since you brought it up, places for the books. We need to figure out how to best use the space so we can get a few more new titles out in the open. I was thinking that if we build a couple shelves with a glass door, we can keep some of the older titles back here in a display case and…what?" Joshua asked after Maggie wrinkled her nose.

"More new titles? Like what?"

"I heard the reviews of *Illegal Death* were good, and that self-help guy on television has a new book out called…"

"*Everyone's Crazy*? Are you serious?" Maggie huffed. "The only people who are going to read that book are the people who watch his show. Do you really want people looking to legitimize their own insanity roaming through the store? I don't think we should be trying to fill the gap of what only a registered psychologist can properly diagnose."

"Margaret, do I need to remind you that we had a great opening night? When was the last time you sold that many books in one day?" Joshua let his hands slap on the sides of his legs.

"Fine. How many do I need to order? Not too many, I hope," Maggie replied.

"No comment about *Illegal Death?*" Joshua said as he pushed past her to go back to the cafe.

"It's not like you are going to listen." Maggie shrugged.

"That's right. Try not to be so personable and charming to our customers, Margaret. We are in this to get people to come here, not scare them away," Joshua said.

"Joshua, you can call me Maggie," Maggie said before he could disappear through their adjoining door.

He stopped and looked at her, but she busied herself with her new books and gently touched the red ribbon he'd used to make them look more like a gift. She didn't see him look her up and down, and had she known what he was thinking, she might have blushed a little. She'd never believe that he was as nervous around her as she was around him.

But before she could catch him, Poe arrived to slink around her feet and purr for her attention. Maggie gave him a good scratch behind the ears before she heard someone jiggling the emergency back door.

Maggie didn't believe that Heath could have somehow gotten out of Sheriff Lee Smith's custody and bravely walked to the back of the shop and turned the doorknob. When she pushed the door open, a wave of cool, misty air hit her face.

"Hello?" she called before peeking around the door to find a familiar person there.

Ruby Sinclair was balancing on one foot as she hopped on the manhole covers three times each then jiggled a couple more knobs, checked a few window ledges, and finally looked at Maggie. With a grand sweep of her arm, Ruby clomped up to Maggie and, with her head high, her chin raised, and her eyes cast down, presented her with a note.

"My father heard about it," she replied and handed Maggie a folded piece of paper before she made her dramatic exit down the alley and around the corner.

Maggie looked at the paper. It was a lovely, dusty lavender color with tiny flowers printed around the edges. When she opened it, it simply said "Thank you for the tea" in the most elegant script Maggie had ever seen.

## About the Author

Harper Lin is a *USA TODAY* bestselling cozy mystery author. When she's not reading or writing mysteries, she loves going to yoga classes, hiking, and hanging out with her family and friends.

For a complete list of her books by series, visit Harper's website.

www.HarperLin.com

Made in the USA
Las Vegas, NV
16 November 2021

34601445R00104